TAURUS DIVIDED

ZODIAC GUARDIANS 4

TAMAR SLOAN
TRICIA BARR

JESS CONNORS PUBLISHING

LOGAN

I s this what being an FBI agent will be like?

Logan narrows his gaze as he does another quick scan of his surroundings, his nose twitching at the stale smell of pizza in his car. He reaches for his binoculars on the seat beside him, digging down into the takeout boxes and empty soda cans they've become buried under.

When the sweep brings up nothing, he sighs, letting the binoculars drop down into his lap. He never thought he'd say it, but he's had enough of burgers, especially when there are never enough napkins. What's more, when they covered surveillance at college, no one mentioned how numb your butt gets after sitting in the same seat for hours on end.

But if Logan's father asked him to stake out this half-built apartment building, then that's exactly what he's going to do. And for as long as it takes. Even though even a stray cat hasn't wandered past all day.

Not when his dad's been preoccupied since the asteroid. It's as if he didn't breathe the sigh of relief the rest of the world did when it was destroyed. In fact, he's been working even longer hours since then.

So, if Logan can help him out by watching a graffiti-covered, completely-deserted building, then he'll do it with a smile and a "yes, sir." No matter how disconcerting pins and needles in his rear end can be.

That's what family does.

The sound of a car has Logan hunching down. He pulls his cap lower over his eyes, seeking out the shadows inside his own car. His pulse trips over itself when the vehicle passes him.

A truck.

Tristan Ayers' truck.

Ayers is driving, with Brielle in the passenger side. Logan crouches down even further, cursing himself. After Brielle noticed him that day outside her house, he knows he needs to be extra careful. He should've sat in the back seat. Surveillance 101—people notice you less if you're not in the front. And it's easier to duck down...

But Brielle is staring straight ahead as the truck rumbles past. Even at this distance Logan can sense her turmoil. It's like a slow moving cement mixer, tumbling and churning no matter how much she wants it to stop.

Logan mentally shakes away the sensation. He'll never feel sympathy for anyone associated with Ayers. She probably feels guilt or regret over the trail of death they've left behind them.

Whatever it is, neither Brielle nor Tristan seems to notice Logan as they continue to the apartment block.

The truck pulls up and three people climb out. It appears what they taught at college is right—Logan missed the fact there must've been someone in the back seat.

Tristan. Brielle. And Veronica's boyfriend head to the front door.

The word *boyfriend* grinds through Logan's mind. How could Veronica do something like this to their dad? Dating someone associated with Tristan is the ultimate betrayal. And after everything their father has done for Logan, betraying him is something he'll never do.

Logan makes a note of the names and their time of arrival as the three disappear inside. He also notes that a door now exists at the entry, something that wasn't there yesterday. It seems Ayers has been doing some home improvements.

Shifting in his seat, Logan waits. And waits. And waits.

No one comes out. No one else arrives. What the hell are they doing in there? Logan cased the joint yesterday, and the interior is little more than a gutted shell.

As time stretches out from minutes to hours, Logan starts to wonder where his sister is. Will she be joining the others in their suspicious hangout? His hands clench around the binoculars. The sting that she chose herself over the foundation that's their family hasn't gone away.

Veronica has always been hot-headed. She's prone to strong emotions—no, fierce emotions. Sometimes they roar through her like a freight train. If she says she loves this Jareth guy, then Logan has no doubt the feeling is a powerful one.

But still… This is their father.

Jack Cadbury's love for his children is the steady, unfailing type. The same Jack felt for Logan and Veronica's mother.

Logan remembers how nervous he was when his mother said she'd met someone. He was five when she told him that she wanted Logan to meet him, too. She assured him that they'd get along, but Logan sensed her edgy uncertainty. He also sensed how much she wanted this to work. It was a desperate tug, deep in her chest.

In the end, her worry was unfounded. Logan could instantly feel Jack's love for his mother. It was the most reassuring feeling Logan had experienced in his young life.

And then it hadn't taken long for that buoyant, comforting sensation to extend to Logan himself. The man who soon became the only father he's ever known loved him unreservedly. Completely. Irrespective of blood or past or future.

Logan will spend his life being grateful Jack Cadbury brought that into his life. And his mother's. It was those emotions that wrapped around her only six years later, when she died of cancer.

The door opening snaps Logan out of his reverie. Sliding down again, he watches over the dash as Ayers and the others climb back into his truck. Jareth—Logan still doesn't like even thinking his name—tries to offer Brielle the front passenger seat, but she shakes her head, and quickly climbs in the back seat, tucking her emotions deep inside of herself.

A few moments later, they drive off.

Logan pushes himself upright and climbs out of the car. Rolling his shoulders, he stretches his neck, enjoying satisfying *cracks* and *pops* as his muscles and joints unfold. Looking at the building, he rubs his chin.

How many of them are aliens? Just Tristan? Or Brielle, too? Even Jareth?

Logan knows his father hasn't crossed Jareth off the potential list. He just has to trust Veronica until he finds out otherwise.

Logan casually wanders over, his gaze darting as he scans his surroundings.

There's no doubt in Logan's mind that aliens exist. Or that Ayers is involved with them. When Logan had told Jack he wanted to be an FBI agent just like him when he was sixteen, his father had looked at him steadily. Then he sat Logan down and calmly outlined what he was really trying to uncover.

That aliens exist. That they pose a threat to Earth. One

far more deadly and destructive than anything Earth has seen yet.

His steady mind and unwavering faith had told Logan all he needed to believe him. Jack didn't think aliens exist, he *knew* they did.

Which is why Logan's here, finally getting some sensation in his backside. To be the one who helps his father show every doubting, sneering, patronizing jackass in the FBI how wrong they are.

At the door, Logan isn't surprised to find it locked, but he is surprised at the high tech keypad. Ayers has put a code on the door. Definitely worthy of note. Tucking his hands in his pockets, Logan continues to wander around the side of the building. All the windows are still boarded up, meaning he can't get a peek inside.

He glances up and freezes for a split-second before he resumes his idle walk, keeping the brim of his cap over his face. There's a camera up above, small and unobtrusive, but a camera, nonetheless.

Continuing around the other side, he sees that there are several of them, set up strategically to cover every inch of the building. Apparently Ayers doesn't want any surprise visitors. Acting shocked when he hits a brick wall about halfway down—even though he knew it was there—Logan turns around, mentally tracking their angles.

Fools. There's a blind spot about four feet down the wall. Tucking away the information for future reference, he heads back to his car like he has all the time in the world. For once, he has some interesting info for his father. Possibly far more than Veronica has been able to glean in her time loitering around Ayers.

Maybe it'll be enough for Dad to let him in, just a little. To trust Logan enough to tell him what's really got his father so rattled.

Hearing a car approaching, Logan quickly climbs into his own. Once again keeping just above the dash, he sees a sleek Mercedes pull in where Ayers was parked not long ago. Logan's eyes widen when a svelte leg slips out, joined by another. A lithe body follows, unfolding until one heck of a blonde bombshell is standing beside the car. Thick waves of buttery hair cascade down her back, and although she's wearing workout gear, Logan's mouth still goes dry. She's all sleek lines and smooth curves.

But it's not just the hotness level that has Logan entranced. Many people experience more than one emotion at a time, but this girl seems to be carrying two of the most contrasting emotions he's ever seen. Simmering, sizzling anger. And sweet, bubbly elation.

The potent mix is fascinating.

She glances over her shoulder and Logan freezes. There's a flash of a porcelain cheek and full, blossom-colored lips, but with a quick flick of a heavy blonde curl, she continues into the building.

Logan manages to snap himself out of his strange daze enough to take a quick photo with his cell as the girl raises her fingers to the keypad. Without a backward glance, she goes inside.

Logan lets out a long breath. Who the hell was that?

Figuring he's about to have another hour or two stuck in his mobile home-away-from-home, he slouches back down only to tense again.

A man appears further down the street wearing dark clothes. He doesn't look left or right as he makes his way to the apartment block.

Now on high alert, Logan reaches for his backpack on the back seat. Not taking his gaze off the man, he pulls it onto his lap and opens it. The man continues toward the front of the building, obviously intent on where he's going.

The moment he reaches into his jacket, Logan slips out of the car. The man draws out a handgun as he presses himself against the door, listening.

Figuring the guy isn't here looking for a cup of sugar, Logan takes a few steps forward so he's standing in the middle of the road. He raises the tranquilizer gun in his hand and clears his throat.

The man startles the moment the sound reaches him. He spins around, his gun looking for a target.

He never has a chance to sight Logan in.

Because Logan has already found his own target.

Just like his father taught him, he locks his muscles, never hesitates.

And pulls the trigger.

2

BRIELLE

The drive back to Mirror Point from "the Gym", as Cassandra calls it, is uncomfortably quiet.

Brielle shifts in the back seat, feeling like the silence and tension in the air physically chafes at her skin no matter how she sits. If her only form of transportation weren't a bike, she'd have come on her own. Anything to avoid being in such close quarters with Tristan just a few days after he openly rejected her.

Again.

After they shared the most amazing kiss the Universe may have ever seen.

The whole thing still confuses her and makes her burn with both longing and anger. She wishes she could just forget it. Move on from this foolish, pointless crush like it never mattered. That would be the best thing for all of them.

It's not like she can just stop seeing Tristan. They have to work together. They're both Zodiac Guardians, and since she was the first one he found, she feels she has a responsibility to their team to put her stupid feelings aside and set an example.

If only it were that easy.

But she's done her best. She hasn't brought up the kiss or their discussion from that night. In fact, she hardly talks to Tristan at all unless she has to. And she showed up for training tonight, even though the thought alone of touching Tristan stabs at her heart. Thankfully, Tristan equally didn't want to touch her because he set it up for both of them to only spar with Jareth, one after the other.

She'd like to believe that's why Jareth is being so quiet. That he's just tired.

But she knows better.

He and Cassandra were there. They saw the kiss. And Jareth has to live with Tristan, so who knows what Tristan might have said to him about Brielle. It's only natural that Jareth would feel awkward being around the two of them together.

If Cassandra had shown up on time, it would have been better. Cassandra adds levity to their quartet. Not to mention that having a fourth sparring partner would have made it less obvious how much Tristan didn't want to be close to Brielle.

Maybe they should fight. It might feel good to punch him.

The thought dies before it can even finish forming in her mind. No. There's no part of her that wants to hurt Tristan. She knows he's doing what he thinks is the right thing, and even though she disagrees, she can still appreciate him being noble over selfish.

Things could be the other way around. He could be a douche and just use her now only to carelessly dump her later, like she's watched happen to countless girls at school.

She looks up at the back of his seat, seeing tufts of dark blond hair brush against the back of his neck.

He has a soulmate. That's what all of this is about. And she should understand that and bow out.

But what if Zarius had it wrong? What if the other Gemini isn't supposed to be a soulmate, but just a partner. Maybe even like a sister. After all, Gemini is the twin sign. Twin, as in siblings. Heck, what if the other Gemini turns out to be a guy?

Brielle can't help but snicker at the idea.

"What's so funny back there?" Jareth looks over his shoulder at her with an almost hopeful expression. Like he's dying for some conversation.

She clears her throat. "Nothing."

He raises a dubious brow, so she mouths, "I'll tell you later," and follows it with a wink.

He smirks and faces forward again.

It's a mercy when they finally pull up at her house.

She gets out and pats the back of Tristan's seat. "Thanks for the ride."

"Of course," he says. "That's what teammates are for."

Brielle rolls her eyes at the back of his head, and as she closes the door, she catches sight of an embarrassed frown forming on Jareth's face. Nice to know it's not just her.

They back out of her driveway and she lets out a sigh as she walks to the front door and heads inside.

"Hi, sweetie," Bea greets with an affectionate smile as she bustles over the stove.

The warm aromas of garlic, oregano and tomatoes tease her nostrils, and her stomach grumbles in response. "Dinner smells amazing!"

"Thanks! It's almost ready." Bea vigorously stirs the contents of the big pot in front of her. "In the meantime, I think Frank wanted to talk to you about something."

"Alright." Brielle hangs her backpack on the coat rack, then goes to the study.

Frank is perusing some papers on his desk, but he looks

up at her when he hears her enter. "Hey, how was your first day back to school?"

She sighs. "Everyone is still going crazy about the asteroid. Even the teachers won't stop talking about it."

"So I take it no actual learning happened, then?" His smile is jovial.

She shrugs. "Oh, I don't know... I did learn that I'm not as interested as everyone else is in the strange ways Tik Tok celebrities tried to protect themselves from the impact. Apparently Justin Bieber hopped into one of those private space shuttles without his wife."

Frank chuckles. "I'm just glad that whole nightmare is over. I know the media is tearing apart the Super Suits, but what no one is saying is that we'd all be dead without them. I, for one, am eternally grateful to whoever's behind those masks."

The sincerity and depth of emotion in Frank's eyes strums a chord in Brielle's heart. For a moment, she feels the urge to tell him the truth. Things would be so much easier if he and Bea knew. She wouldn't have to keep telling them half-truths about what she's doing with Tristan and the others.

The night of the asteroid, they'd been so worried, calling and calling to see where she was. And she couldn't answer. Not only because she was flying into space to rescue Cassandra, but because she couldn't lie to them, especially not before they may all die. She had to wait until the asteroid had been destroyed to give them any kind of explanation, which was flimsy at best.

And yet, they didn't grill her. They never pushed her for answers. They took what she said at face value. Somehow, that makes her feel worse. That they put so much trust in her, and she's hiding this huge secret life from them.

But then, what would they do if they did know the truth?

That she's an alien orphan freak with powers, living under their roof and putting them at constant risk. Maybe they wouldn't be so trusting then. Maybe they'd undo the adoption, send her back like a defective product.

No, she can never tell them. They're safer not knowing. And so is she.

"So, Bea said you wanted to talk about something?"

"Yes." He smooths his hands across the papers on his desk. "All this asteroid business has caused such a massive backlog for us. So many clients pulled all their money out, others just wanted their funds moved, and now the same clients who pulled their money want to reinvest..." He throws his hands up and shakes his head. "It's all just causing a huge paper pile up for the company. So, I was hoping to hire you as a kind of intern. You could help us get caught up on all this mess, and it would be something official that would look great on your college resume."

"Yes!" she bursts. "I'd love to help you in any way I can!"

"I was hoping you'd say that." Frank smiles wide, his brow smoothing in relief.

Her insides are bubbling with excitement. "When do I start?"

"How about after dinner?" he suggests.

"Sounds great!"

Brielle beams at him. This won't make it up to Frank for hiding her secret from him, but it's something she can do to really help.

3

CASSANDRA

Cassandra enters the apartment building—which she's come to refer to as "the Gym"—a sense of anxiety building like the rumble of a volcano. She tosses her shoulder bag on the metal folding chair, ready to blow some garbage to smithereens!

Today was a rough day.

School opened for the first time since the asteroid incident a few days ago, and all anyone was talking about was the people in suits who "saved the world". Memes all over social media, conspiracy theories, rumors about the possible faces behind the masks, which of course, everyone assumes are powerful celebrities. The most ridiculous rumor she heard was that the suits were actually robots designed by Bill Gates like he's some real life Tony Stark.

Cassandra shakes her head. Ugh, and Suki wouldn't shut up about wanting the pink Iron Man suit. *I mean, come on. For one, we're way more awesome than Iron Man. And two, no offense to Brielle, but my gold suit is way hotter.*

But nobody should be talking about this at all! Cassandra may have saved the planet—okay, yeah, she still feels pretty awesome about that—but she exposed them in the process. She should have been more careful. If she had stuck around long enough for them to all make a plan rather than trying to be all righteous and heroic, they might not have been seen. And if the world discovers who they are, they'll have more than Skins and Chardis to worry about.

Raising her hand toward a fresh pile of black garbage bags collected from the neighborhood, she unleashes her fury in the form of a photon blast, instantly incinerating the pile to ash.

She smiles. The destruction is so oddly satisfying. Plus, there's also the fact that she's helping the neighborhood and the environment by cleanly getting rid of rubbish. No emissions. No residue. Just ash.

Much better. After all, the day wasn't a total loss. Her father didn't come home again today. He's been staying at his office ever since the night she stood up to him, supposedly because the changing market caused by the non-destruction of the planet has kept him very busy.

And the truth is, she doesn't miss him. From the moment she stopped caring about his judgment, stopped striving to be the person he wanted her to be, life has been so much easier. Like this huge weight has been lifted off her shoulders. And now that she has her eyes wide open, it's refreshing not to be smothered by his overbearing presence. Maybe all this time away will make him realize he's been a terrible father.

Before Cassandra can aim her glowing hand at her next target, her phone buzzes in the pocket of her workout jacket. She pulls it out, hoping for yet more distraction from her fretful thoughts.

It's a notification that Suki tagged her in a video on Insta. Cassandra taps the video.

As soon as she sees news anchor Sofia Simmons on the screen, she wishes she hadn't.

"NASA satellites were able to catch this stunning yet confusing footage of the asteroid explosion," Sofia reports. A little box to the right of her head displays footage of an unknown golden suited figure expelling blinding light at the asteroid, which irrefutably is what destroyed it, while three other suited figures float on the sidelines.

Cassandra scowls at her phone. The army of Skins they were fighting have been conveniently left out. *Invisible assholes.*

"United States officials have no idea who the suited figures are, and no other country's government has come forward to accept responsibility. As the footage was captured over U.S. airspace before the seemingly inevitable impact, the assumption is that the responsible party was from our own soil. Both NASA and the FBI are investigating the—"

Crack!

Cassandra jumps, dropping her phone and silencing the fashionable, although irritating at the moment, Sofia.

What the hell was that? It sounded like a gunshot.

Scanning every inch of the inside of the building, she slowly kneels down to pick up her phone, then stands back up. She takes a quick glance at it. Luckily, the bedazzled rose gold case protected it from damage.

She has to figure out what that sound was. This is a shady neighborhood, so it could be some gang activity. Or it could just be some dumb kid playing with a gun because he thinks it makes him cool. Either way, she needs to find out.

Because it could also be a Skin. Although, if it is, wouldn't that bullet have been meant for her?

She rushes to the computer screen in the far corner that displays the feeds from every camera they have around the building. She carefully inspects each box, but nothing is amiss. Not that that means much; each camera only captures the immediate six-foot radius from their respective walls. If she wants to investigate further, she'll have to go outside.

The supposed shot sounded like it came from the front of the building. Bracing herself for a fight, she cracks open the back door and peeks outside. There doesn't seem to be anyone around, so she silently squeezes out, securely closing the door behind her without a sound. Stepping as lightly as she can, she creeps around the edge of the building, keeping to the shadows for protection.

Putting her hands in front of her like weapons ready to shoot, she scales toward the front of the building. As she gets closer, she sees two figures moving in the middle of the road.

She freezes, holds her breath, and watches intently.

One figure is dragging the other to the opposite side of the road. The latter figure isn't putting up a fight. In fact, it's completely limp.

Her hand rushes to her mouth. *Omigod, is he dead?!*

The first figure reaches his apparent destination—the silver sedan she noticed earlier. She didn't think anyone had been inside. He leans his victim against the rear left tire and, taking a suspicious glance around, opens his trunk. Deciding he hasn't been seen, he hoists the body into the empty space.

Then he closes the trunk, rounds the car to the driver's side, gets in, and drives away.

Cassandra is left hugging the mortar, wondering in horror what the hell just happened.

After a few moments of petrification, she picks up her phone and dials Tristan.

"You're not going to believe what I just saw!"

4

VERONICA

Veronica picks up after the second ring. "Well, hello hot-boyfriend-of-mine."

"Hello, amazing-girl-who-should've-run-by-now," Jareth jokes back.

Veronica giggles. "You're stuck with me, no matter what. What's up?"

"Nothing. I'm just on my way home from the cemetery."

"How was your visit?" she asks warmly.

"I told them all about my flight training." She can almost see the playful lilt of his eyebrows.

"Did your mum agree that you should be taking me, too?"

Veronica didn't bat an eye when he told her he still speaks to his parents. Instead, she'd slipped her arms around his waist and tucked herself in close, pointing out that they're still very much alive in his mind and heart, so of course he would. Jareth's hug had been extra tight after those words.

He chuckles. "There's no way I'm mentioning you're insisting on coming. She'd think it's a fabulous idea."

She pouts as if the gesture would still affect Jareth over the phone. "No fair."

"But safe," he points out.

"Speaking of parents," Veronica huffs again, blankly staring at the entertainment center in front of her while the TV entertains itself. "I'm just waiting for Dad to come home."

Jareth's brows contract a little. "How are things with him?"

She sighs. "I haven't learned a thing since the asteroid. He's holding his cards close to his chest, as they say." And it's what's on those cards that they really need to see.

"All you can do is be ready for when he wants to share, I suppose," he suggests.

Veronica pauses, swallowing before she can ask the question that's been on her mind for days. "Do you think he doesn't trust me anymore?"

"Your dad has never been one to share his theories until he's sure, has he?"

Veronica sighs. "Yeah, that's true." The fact that her dad shouldn't be trusting her is the clincher, and she knows that.

"Why don't we go for a picnic on the weekend?" Jareth offers.

"Ooh!" Veronica says, anticipation returning the lilt to her voice. "At the usual place?"

"In a sea of daisies," he promises.

"Best. Date. Ever."

It's one they've had before, and one they'll have again. They tuck into a corner of Alden's back garden, one that's little more than an expanse of lawn—so no one can sneak up on the house, as Tristan told them—surrounded by a high brick wall. There, they spread out a blanket and whatever delicious treat Brielle's left in the fridge. And then Jareth weaves a magical garden around them, one comprising entirely of daisies of every shape and color.

Jareth chuckles. "I'm looking forward to it."

The sound of the door opening carries down the hall.

"Gotta go," Veronica says, her voice subdued. "Dad's home."

"Maybe just hang out with him for a change?" Jareth suggests. "Forget that you're dating a Zodiac Guardian for a little while?"

"Maybe you're right." She huffs. "About just hanging out with him, that is. I'm not just dating a Zodiac Guardian, I'm in love with a Zodiac Guardian."

"And that Zodiac Guardian loves you," he says.

"Kitkat, I'm home, and I come bearing pizza!" calls Veronica's dad as he comes in the front door.

Veronica sits up from her lounging position on the couch and looks curiously in that direction, tucking her cell phone into her pocket. *Pizza? And what's up with his cheery voice?*

"What's the occasion?" she asks, half teasing, half suspicious.

He comes into the living room and sets the steaming pizza box on the coffee table. The smells of gooey cheese and spicy pepperoni make her mouth water.

"What do you mean?" he asks, sitting down on the couch beside her and popping open a can of Pepsi.

"You're home before nine *and* you brought me pizza," she replies with her trademark snark. "If I didn't know any better, I'd think you were about to bribe me."

He chuckles, takes a sip of his soda, then reaches forward to open the box, letting the aromatic heat escape in a puff. She doesn't miss the fact that he doesn't make eye contact, which only makes her more suspicious.

"Alright, Dad, spill it," she demands, crossing her arms and legs and narrowing her eyes on him.

He picks up a slice of pizza, strings of cheese reluctantly stretching apart as he lifts it to his mouth. He takes a bite then blows out air with his mouth full to cool the too-hot food. "I don' know 'uht you're dalkin' 'bout," he says around the food still cradled on his tongue.

"You've been working late every single night since the asteroid," Veronica explains. "And you expect me to believe that, out of nowhere, you just happen to get off work at a normal time and decide to pick up pizza for the two of us to eat together like an actual family?" She shakes her head. "No, it's too weird. I don't buy it. So I'll say again, spill, mister."

Her dad chews and swallows, then wipes his mouth with a napkin, giving her a knowing look. "You're just like your mother." He sighs. "You got me. There is something I wanted to tell you, and I'd hoped that the pizza would butter you up before I did. Could you at least take a bite first?"

Without looking away from him, she picks up a slice and takes a bite, flaring her brow as she chews despite the obvious discomfort from the heat. She swallows and juts her chin at him in invitation.

He shuffles in place, then checks his wrist watch. "Well, I guess it's about that time anyway." When he looks back up at her, his face shows his age and stress. "What I'm about to tell you may be hard to hear at first, but I need you to know it's for the best."

Which means there's no way it's going to be good. "What is it, Dad?" The edge to her voice is sharp.

"Okay, I'm just gonna say it. We're bringing in your boyfriend for questioning."

She shoots to her feet. "What?"

"We have reason to believe that he was involved with the asteroid explosion," he explains.

The outrage is automatic and overwhelming. So is the panic. "W—you—how could you think that?" she demands, frazzled. "What *reason* do you have to believe that?!"

"He's Tristan Ayers' best friend and roommate," her dad

says flatly, as if that should explain it all. "We've been watching both of them for a long time and—"

"Don't you think I would know if my boyfriend were capable of something like that?" she cuts him off. "I mean, come on, these are teenagers, not international terrorists!"

"Well, the truth is, when you're young and in love, you don't have the best judgment," he reasons, rubbing the scruff on his chin.

"Oh, so now my judgment is in question?" she snaps. She crosses her arms again and shakes her head. "I knew you didn't trust me."

"Honestly, I don't!" he blurts, standing now, too.

She lets her jaw fall and gasps loudly.

"I think you've been hiding things from me," he continues. "I think you're in way over your head with this boy and you'd say and do anything to protect him."

"You're damn right I would!" she says. "I love him! You can't bring him in!"

They stare angrily at each other for a long moment.

He puts out his hand, palm up. "Give me your phone."

She takes a step back and turns her body away, protecting the pocket her cell is hiding in. "No!"

"Give. Me. Your. Phone!" he barks. "I won't have you warning him."

She tries to make a run for her room, but he grabs her and yanks the phone out of her pocket.

"No, no!" she screams, scrambling to try to retrieve it.

But he's so much bigger and stronger than her. It only takes a minute for her to realize the struggle is futile.

She throws her hands down and stomps a rebellious foot. "If you do this, I will never speak to you again."

"It's already done," he says, taking her phone apart and stashing the pieces in separate pockets on his person. "They should get him any minute."

Her entire body is shaking with fury, betrayal, desperation to save Jareth. "You have no idea how big a mistake you're making!"

His phone rings, and he brings it to his ear without breaking eye contact with her. "Okay, I'll be right there." Then he puts it back in his pocket and heads for the door.

"Please, Dad, don't do this!" she pleads, following him to the door.

"Someday, when this is all over, you'll see that I was right, and maybe you'll forgive me," he says before leaving the apartment and closing the door behind him.

Veronica slams her hands against the door, fighting the tears that threaten.

She's not going to let him do this. It might not be too late.

Hooking her messenger bag over her shoulder—and grabbing a spiteful piece of pizza for the road—she heads out the door, determined to find Jareth before it's too late.

5

JARETH

Jareth's being followed.

He pulls his head down and his shoulders up as he leaves the cemetery and takes a sharp right. He came here after leaving the Gym with Tristan and Brielle, needing a break from the constant tension that now exists between the two.

He'd noticed the white sedan was there when he arrived, taking Tristan's advice to always be aware of his surroundings. And now, the sedan is conveniently leaving at the same time he is.

All the comfort he worked hard to draw around himself while he sat by his parents' memorial dissolves, and the tense uneasiness returns. The feeling bloomed as he watched the footage of the Zodiacs destroy the asteroid, and hasn't gone away since. Who knows what it's going to mean now that they've been seen, but it can't be good.

Just like the white sedan that also turns the corner isn't giving him any positive vibes.

Picking up his pace, Jareth jams his hands in his pockets

There are Feds or Skins in that car, and he's not sure which he prefers.

As the corner of the next block appears ahead, Jareth's fingers twitch nervously in his pockets. Continue home as quickly as possible? Or take the longer route, and see if he can lose the tail?

Making a snap decision, he goes left. The opposite direction will take him to the house he shares with Tristan. He hears the car accelerate, and his own pulse increases. His right hand wraps around his cell. Tristan programmed a panic button into it. All he has to do is press three numbers in the order he was shown.

To his surprise, the white car powers straight past him, the two men in the front seats not even glancing at Jareth. His pace slows as he watches the car turn at the next intersection. In a disbelieving blink, it's gone.

Jareth huffs out a breath. The old fear that he's getting paranoid tickles his consciousness. Now that he knows the enormity of the evil they're facing, it's hard not to see danger at every corner.

Probably because danger *could* be at any corner.

For a moment, he considers calling Veronica back. He draws his cell out of his pocket, needing to give his anxiety levels a break. Hers is the other number that he can dial without even glancing at his phone. The other number that will give him the sense that he's safe. That everything can be all right in this world.

But before his finger can press the buttons, Jareth looks up. He tucks the phone back in his pocket and frowns.

The white car is waiting at the other end of the block.

The tight, anxious fear is back, gripping him like a monstrous serpent. It leaves Jareth frozen, even his shallow breaths feeling like too much. He is most certainly, undeniably being followed.

Feds. Or Skins.

Tristan's voice follows straight after with two more possibilities. *Run. Or fight.*

Except Jareth's muscles are locked. Tristan forgot there was a third option. *Freeze.*

And then it's his mother's turn. *Take the hard road. Every time.*

The hours the Zodiacs have spent in the Gym start to flash through Jareth's mind. In theory, he has everything he needs to take the hard road. Time to channel his inner Tristan. And Veronica and Brielle and Cassandra. And every other Zodiac who's waiting to be discovered.

Snapping out of his self-imposed freeze, Jareth strides forward. With each step, his pace lengthens and fills with purpose. It's time to get some answers.

The man in the driver's seat is making a show of being on his cell when Jareth knocks on the window. Before Jareth knows what's happened, both men storm out of the car.

"Step back," the driver shouts, his hand tucked into his jacket.

Jareth does as he's told, the fear spiking, but strangely under control. "If I tell you to stop following me, will you afford me the same respect?"

The second man comes up beside the first. "Come in with us and answer some questions and you've got a deal."

So, they're feds.

Jareth crosses his arms. "No, thanks."

The first man's nostrils flare with irritation. "We know you have something to hide. Anyone associated with Ayers does."

Jareth cocks his head. "Did Jack send you?"

"Why don't you come with us?" the second fed offers with a snarl. "We'll ask our questions. You ask yours."

"No, thanks," Jareth repeats as he takes another step backward. "I don't intend on ever going with you."

In some ways, these men are just as dangerous to the Zodiacs as Skins. They want the Zodiacs off the map just as much as Chardis does.

The feds glance at each other. The first adjusts his jacket, and it opens enough for Jareth to get a glimpse of the gun holstered at the man's hip. He grins coldly. "It's cute you thought you have a choice."

The two men lunge simultaneously just as the words hit Jareth's consciousness. He leaps back, but it's too late. One of the feds grabs his arm and jerks, spinning Jareth around. Before he knows what's happened, his arm is twisted painfully behind him and the fed is grappling to bring his other arm back.

Jareth struggles with all his might, but the feds are expecting that, no doubt trained in handling those who resist arrest. There's a clink of metal and Jareth realizes they're getting handcuffs out.

He fights harder, yanking as he tries to get his hands free, even though it hurts. He kicks backward, feeling a flash of satisfaction as his foot hits a leg, eliciting a grunt from the fed. But then he's being spun around and slammed against the side of the car. The air is knocked out of Jareth's lungs as he hits hard metal, his face roughly pressed onto the hood.

"I'm happy to do this the hard way," the fed growls in Jareth's ear.

Jareth stops moving, ignoring the satisfied chuckle behind him.

He can't fight off two federal agents. Especially considering he can't use his powers to create a weapon of some sort —doing so would give them irrefutable evidence the Zodiacs aren't from Earth.

Although, maybe he doesn't need a weapon...

Jareth yanks his head up as far as he can considering the palm holding it down. "No, Tristan! They're feds!"

Both men pause and Jareth continues to stare at the end of the street.

"Run!" he shouts.

The image of Tristan turns and breaks into a sprint, disappearing around the corner. The second fed breaks into a run after him, drawing out his gun.

"Stop or I'll shoot," he calls out.

Jareth almost rolls his eyes. If the fool knew Tristan at all he would've realized this is nothing but an illusion. Tristan would never run if a Zodiac was in trouble.

But he doesn't have time. Just like he doesn't have time to imagine the man's shock when he rounds the corner and there's no Tristan in sight. Or to chuckle at the thought of the fed scouring every yard, hiding spot or escape route, certain in the knowledge that no one can disappear into thin air.

Because Jareth has his own escape to pull off.

The fed still holding him shoves Jareth as if to remind him he's still here. "Two in one day," he growls victoriously. "The boss will be happy."

Jareth doesn't respond, waiting for the right moment. It comes a second later, the cold hard sensation of steel being pressed to his wrist.

"Did you know arachnophobia is one of the most common fears?" he asks casually.

"What?"

Jareth closes his eyes as he mentally pictures what the feds are about to see. He projects the image of a spider, the biggest, hairiest one he can conjure, and has it streak down his arm. Straight to the fed's hands as he tries to cuff him.

"What the hell?" the fed shouts, instinctively jumping backward.

Which is all Jareth needs. He spins, his fist already following through and punches the fed in the face. Pain radiates through his hand and up his arm, but the strike does what he needs it to do. The fed hits the ground, instantly trying to get back up only to fall back onto his side.

Jareth doesn't wait to see how quickly the man is going to recover. He runs in the opposite direction the first man left, following the apparition of Tristan.

As he sprints away, he realizes that if he wasn't wanted by the FBI before, then he is now.

But it's more than that.

The fact that they were bringing him in for questioning means Jack no longer trusts his daughter.

6

TRISTAN

The headlights on Tristan's truck illuminate the dirt road ahead of him as he bounces over it. Reaching over, he turns up the air conditioner. He's felt a permanent sense of suffocating heat from the moment they learned about the Zodiac footage.

Or maybe he's just had an elevated body temperature since the kiss…

Shaking his head, Tristan tightens his hold on the steering wheel. How could everything have gone so wrong after a moment that felt so right? They may have saved Earth from Chardis's attack, but humans know they exist. The FBI are sniffing around as if they suspect they're close.

Because they are.

And Skins are going to be everywhere, waiting for a sign of Zodiac life. Knowing there are now four of them.

Tristan's hands reflexively clench and unclench around the steering wheel and he wonders if it's possible to snap it. So much tension is wound through him, it's only a matter of time before something has to give.

Especially considering the feds and Skins are only the

cherry on this crap-cake. The wormhole is still sitting there, waiting to spit out its next evil surprise.

Hell, it could be Chardis itself.

And Tristan thought the best thing to do was kiss Brielle. The one person he never wants to see hurt. Adding layers of awkwardness on top awkwardness whenever the Zodiacs are together. He's seen the way Jareth acts like a turtle wanting to disappear into his shell. The way he and Veronica avoid touching, as if it's now illegal. The way Cassandra keeps jamming her hands on her hips in annoyance. Could he screw this up anymore?

Seeing the gate to the Pierces' property, Tristan pulls over and kills the lights. He needs to talk to Brielle. He needs to tell her what he's decided.

He needs to find a way to fix this.

Creeping down the driveway, he notes that the kitchen and dining room lights are out, while the bedrooms are lit up. Good, he was hoping they'd all be getting ready for bed.

Making his way around the back, memories flood Tristan's mind. It feels like yesterday and yet a lifetime ago that he snuck down this path, on his way to warn Brielle that Skins were coming.

That was the night she learned the truth about Zodiacs.

That was when he'd still hoped she was his soulmate.

Clenching his jaw, Tristan makes his way through the shrubs down the side of the house and into the backyard. Those thoughts are what got him into the pickle he's in. Which means they need to stop. Brielle and soulmate can no longer be two words anywhere near the same vicinity as each other.

Looking up, he sees movement in her window. Grabbing his cell, he sends her a quick text.

Could we talk?

Her reply is almost instant. *You want to talk? To me?*

Frowning, he types out a reply. *Yes, with you.*

But you've been proactively avoiding doing that.

His jaw is so tight that he wonders whether his teeth are fusing together from the pressure. *I know. I'm sorry. That's why I thought we should talk.*

There's a pause. *Sure. Where and when?*

Your backyard. How about now?

A second later, Brielle's window slides open and she leans out, scanning the shadowy backyard. Tristan steps onto an open patch of grass and waves. Brielle seems to pause, as if she can't quite believe he's there. A second later, she closes the window and disappears.

Tristan steps back into the safety of the shrub, wishing he had a steering wheel to clench. Maybe snap.

This conversation isn't going to be easy.

The back door opens, then shuts with a soft *click*. Brielle streaks across the porch and onto the lawn, lithe and light-footed. Unerringly, she finds him in the corner of the garden, coming to stand in front of him.

"Tristan?" she asks, confused and cautious.

Tristan blinks. Brielle's in her pyjamas. A tank top and shorts that give meaning to the word 'short'. Even though it's dark, the outline of her curves are enough for his imagination to fill in the rest. The moment in the car, the near-kiss, rises in his mind. The time she was almost wearing less than she is now...

His body temperature spikes all over again.

"That's what you sleep in?" he half-squeaks.

Brielle looks down. "On warm nights, yes."

Dammit. He should've come in winter.

She crosses her arms. "What's wrong with it?"

Wiping his hand down his face, Tristan acknowledges he's not starting well. "Nothing. Ignore me. I came here to tell you that Cassandra saw a guy shoot another outside the Gym, then she saw him stash the body in the boot."

Brielle gasps, taking a small step forward. "Is she okay?"

"Yeah, she laid low and called me. By the time I got there, no one was in sight."

"Poor Cassie." Brielle's hand flutters to her throat. "It might've been the guy who's been following us."

"Maybe. The security cameras didn't catch anything, so we don't know if it was feds or Skins."

Or both. McNary proved how deeply the Skins have infiltrated the FBI.

Brielle thinks this over for a long moment. "Thanks for telling me. We really do need to be on high alert."

"We really do. That's why I'm here." Tristan clears his throat. "I wanted to let you know that keeping you safe is the most important thing to me."

In this world. Actually, in the Universe.

"Oh, Tristan—"

"So, I wanted to check that you're okay. You know, after...everything."

It's Brielle's turn to blink. "You're checking if I'm okay?" she asks softly.

Tristan's eyes close for the briefest of seconds. This is so much harder than kicking a bunch of Skins asses so they can save Earth. "Yeah. First we had the asteroid. Next, we're all over the news. Now, we're being followed with shots being fired. There's a lot of heat on the Zodiacs right now."

Brielle's body softens, which only seems to accentuate the curves Tristan is working really hard not to look at. "Actually, I've had good news."

"Yeah?"

"Frank, I mean Dad, asked me to intern with his company."

"That's not good news, that's great news!" Brielle would

love feeling like she's helping the people who gave her what she always wanted—a family.

It also means she'll be spending more time with them. It only cements Tristan's decision even more.

"Thanks, Tristan." She takes a step forward. "I know things have been…awkward. But—"

Tristan's retreat is immediate. And his step is twice the size. A branch spears into his back, but he welcomes the pain. Part of him wishes the shrub was a cactus.

"I need you to be safe, Brielle," he says hoarsely. "It's why I've decided we need to be apart for a while."

"What?" she gasps. "Apart? Why?"

"So we can lay low. No more training at the Gym. No more Zodiac activity unless absolutely necessary. We need to get the feds off our backs. To throw the Skins off our scent."

"You weren't checking I'm okay," she says softly, almost as if she's feeling betrayed. "You were reminding me what we're up against." Despite the lack of light, Brielle's frown is unmistakable. "You've really thought this through."

He's thought of nothing else, hating the solution as much as she seems to. But it will keep her safe. Away from him.

And it gives Tristan time to get his wayward emotions under control and focus on the Zodiacs.

"You've got a family, Brielle. School. Now, a job you're excited about. Enjoy normality for a change. Show the world there's nothing worth keeping an eye on."

"You're running," Brielle states flatly. She takes a step forward. "This is because we ki—"

"No!" Aware he half-shouted the word, Tristan modulates his tone. "This is about keeping you and everyone else safe."

"I don't know why you think pushing me away is going to solve this," she says angrily.

Tristan slips out from the bush, no longer able to have her

in such close proximity. "I'm doing this for the Zodiacs. That's my job, Brielle."

"And what about you, Tristan?" She sags, as if the anger just rushed out. "What about us?"

The first question, he can answer. The Zodiacs come first.

The second question slams him in the gut like a wrecking ball. The existence of the Zodiacs is what deeply connects them.

And yet will mean they can never be together.

Tristan steps back, then takes another. "There can be no us, remember?" he asks softly, the words feeling like they just shredded his tongue.

Brielle stills, becoming a shadowy statue. They hold there for long moments, surrounded by nightfall and emotion so thick it clogs his ability to breathe.

The moment Brielle moves, bringing her hand up to her mouth, Tristan turns and leaves. As he strides, every muscle locked so he doesn't turn around and go back, he pretends his keen sense of hearing can't detect the soft sobs trailing behind him.

The anger, he could handle.

The crying slices at his heart.

7

LOGAN

Unconscious bodies are heavy. That's another thing they haven't covered in college.

Logan grunts as he drags the dead weight through the back door of the address his father gave him.

"It's an FBI safe-house," he'd told Logan when he'd said there was something he wanted to show him. "I'll meet you there."

The single-story house is at the end of a quiet cul-de-sac. Even though there's no one in sight, Logan's keen to be out of view. Quickly checking for a pulse, and finding one, he rolls the body through and shuts the door behind him.

He didn't tell his father exactly what he had for show and tell, uncomfortable with sharing that sort of information over the phone, but his father got the gist it was important. Maybe it was Logan's panting breaths after lugging the unconscious man into the trunk of his car. Maybe it was the way he gritted his teeth the whole time they spoke, tense with the fear that this guy could die.

Or maybe it was the words Logan used. "You need to see something."

Either way, Jack had instantly said he was on his way.

Inside the house, Logan finds himself in the kitchen. Leaving the man just inside the door, he rushes to the drawers, hoping to find something to tie him up with. His brows shoot up when he finds duct tape and scissors in the top drawer where cutlery is supposed to be. The term 'safe house' is obviously a loose one...

Hauling the man into a chair, Logan sets about taping him in. He wraps the silver material around the man's chest, legs, and hands. Remembering that this guy had a gun, Logan adds several more layers around his wrists for good measure.

With that finished, Logan steps back to survey his handiwork. The man's strapped tightly to the chair, his head lolling forward. The sedative has done exactly what it's supposed to do—neutralize him without killing him. This way he can answer some questions.

Now all Logan has to do is wait.

Hands on his hips, he looks around. The house is neat and clean, pretty bare...and quiet. He frowns as the silence grows, beginning to feel oppressive. The man moans, and Logan senses his consciousness returning, along with a hint of pain and confusion.

Not wanting to feel anything from this man who they're going to have to interrogate, Logan looks around again, noting the TV on the wall above the nearby dining table. Excellent. A distraction.

The remote sits on the table so Logan turns the TV on, and a news channel flickers to life. A blonde woman sits behind a desk, three bold words trailing across the bottom of the screen on a loop.

Superheroes or Superthreats?

The image cuts to a guy with an impressive set of dreadlocks. He throws his arms in the air as if he's in a church. "We don't know who you are, Suited Saviors, but we thank you!"

he shouts. "We worship you!" he shouts even louder. "We are yours to command!"

Logan snorts, feeling the man's fevered adoration from here. He's about to turn it off again when the image cuts back to the news anchor.

"As you can see, the support for our mystery asteroid destroyers is only growing," she says. "Of course, those feelings aren't unanimous."

The screen fills again, this time with a woman in a dark suit and a tight bun. "There are countless questions people should be asking themselves," she says sharply. "Who are these people? Where do they come from? Suits like the ones they're wearing belong in a science-fiction book, not our world." She leans forward toward whoever is interviewing her, face tighter than her bun. "Has anyone considered they're more dangerous than the asteroid itself?"

The door opens, making Logan jump, and his father comes through.

"They sure as hell are more dangerous than the asteroid."

His father shuts the door then stops, his eyebrows hiking up into his non-existent hairline.

"The thing you found is a guy?"

Logan nods. "He was snooping around the apartment building." While the blonde girl was in there. "With a gun."

His father walks over to the man and lifts his head by his hair. "And you tranquilized him," he observes.

"Yes, sir. Thought we could ask him a few questions."

His father drops the man's head, eliciting a soft groan. He looks at Logan, his gaze assessing. Logan holds still, despite the happiness bubbling in his gut. He can sense his father's soft pride.

He grunts. "Impressive, son." The man in the chair groans again. "Let's see if he has any answers, shall we?"

Before Logan can blink, his father draws his hand back

and slaps it across the man's face. Logan bites down on his gasp, unprepared for the violence.

The man moans again, his head lolling from the impact.

"He's really out of it," murmurs Logan, trying to keep his cool. This is his chance to prove himself.

"Or, he's faking."

Another hit and Logan's not sure his father's right. The man's pain feels muted, somehow. Disconnected.

His father draws his hand for another slap when the man raises his head. Logan notes with shock that it's clear, cold eyes that scan the room. The muscles in the man's shoulders and neck contract and release as he tests his bonds.

He was definitely awake.

Logan's father steps in closer. "Who are you?"

The man's gaze barely flickers over Jack, then Logan, instead focusing on his surroundings. "Where am I?"

"A short pit stop before prison," Logan's father says flatly. "Now, what were you doing outside the apartment block?"

The man's muscles flex again, his upper lip curling in frustration. His arms twitch.

"There's no point," Logan tells him. "You're strapped in for the ride."

The man inflates his chest, the lines of duct tape stretching. Logan senses the man's hard determination a second before he yanks his arms. Suddenly, he's standing, his hands by his side, shredded gray tape hanging from his body. A grunt and a jerk and he frees his legs, too.

Logan's father leaps back as he simultaneously withdraws his gun. "Get behind me, Logan!"

Logan stumbles as he does what he's told, shocked that the man could simply snap out of his bindings. It's like it was nothing but sticky tape!

"Stop, or I'll shoot!" his father warns.

The man straightens, making no move toward them. His hand slips into his jacket pocket.

Logan's father's hand tightens around his gun, his voice hiking. "Keep your hands where I can see them!"

The man ignores him and Logan braces himself for the gunshot. The man's hand appears, no gun in sight, and rises swiftly to his mouth.

Since he came across the man, Logan registers the first flash of fear in him, small and desperate, like a child demanding to be noticed. There's the slightest flicker of his eyelids as he places a pill on his tongue then crunches down.

"Chardis is coming and there's nothing any of you can do about it," he growls.

His eyes roll back in his head as he crumples, pink-tinged saliva frothing at the edges of his mouth.

Shocked silence fills the room as Logan's father slips his gun back into his hip holster and closes his jacket again. He nudges the man with his foot. Logan doesn't need to touch the man to know he's dead. He's never felt this level of... nothing from someone. The man's inner world is silent.

His mind a whirl, Logan turns to his father. "Who's Chardis?"

Rubbing his bald head, his father sighs. "I don't know. I haven't heard the term before." His lips press together. "But I bet someone else has."

Tristan Ayers.

Even if Logan wasn't aware of his father's theories, following Ayers for the past few weeks would've told him there's something suspicious about the guy. Living in a house that's more fortress than home without parents. Variable school attendance. And hanging out in an abandoned apartment block that has security installed, doing who knows what.

Logan swallows, his gaze sliding away from the dead man. "What do we do with him?"

"I'll organize a clean-up crew." His father squints at him. "How you doing? This was one hell of an introduction to…"

"To your world," Logan finishes. He nods toward the man. "I taped him up good. He should never have been able to break through those bonds. And whatever he knew, he was willing to take the information to the grave."

His father nods solemnly. "This is dangerous, Logan. We're not up against the usual bad guys."

Aliens.

Suited threats with powers they can only guess at.

His father waits, and Logan knows this is his moment to make a decision. There's no course that can prepare him for what he would face. There's no doubt this will be life or death, for him and many others. He's either in…or out.

Logan throws back his shoulders. There's no way he's letting the man who raised him as his own fight this alone. "I want to learn, Dad. You were right. Everything depends on defeating these monsters."

The pride this time is sharper, deeper, sweeter. It's everything Logan's ever wanted.

His father nods. "It's time you joined us."

Us? Logan's pulse trips at the word. Who is us?

His father holds the door open. "Come on. There's something I need to show you."

8

VERONICA

The lights in the convenience store down the street are bright, an uncomfortable contrast to the darkness Veronica just ran through to get here, but she doesn't give her eyes time to adjust.

She runs straight for the rack of cheap cell phones, her fingers fumbling with them at random as her eyes scan for the lowest priced burner phone. She only has a handful of one dollar bills in her bag, and she hopes it's enough. Finding the crappiest flip phone she's ever seen—they still make these?—she grabs it and dashes to the counter.

The clerk lazily takes the phone and scans it, the wait making Veronica tap her foot impatiently.

"Six-thirty," he mumbles, completely clueless to what's at stake.

She fiddles around in her bag, gathering the small handful of dollar bills. There are only five. She digs around at the bottom, certain there's some change floating around. There has to be!

Her fingers find the smooth metal coins and she gathers them up, pulling them out to count them.

Twenty-five, fifty, seventy-five, eighty-five, ninety-five, ninety-six, ninety-seven. *Dammit!* There's not enough!

Her eyes flicker across the counter, searching for loose change. She spies a quarter and nickel in the basin of the change dispenser and grabs it. She slaps the money onto the counter, snatches the phone and darts out the door before the clerk can realize he's been shorted. *Three cents is not that big a deal*, she tells herself.

As soon as she rounds the corner, she rips the package open and powers up the phone. Luckily, she knows Jareth's number by heart and dials it in.

Pressing the phone to her ear, she whispers, "Pick up, Jareth. Pick up!"

The phone rings several times, then goes straight to voicemail.

Dammit!

What if they already got him? No, that can't be. That just can't be!

She calls him again, pacing the alley behind the store as she painstakingly listens to one ring after another.

Still no answer.

With rapid fingers she types:

J, it's V. Dad took my phone. If you get this, please call me asap!

She stares at the phone unblinkingly after she hits send, praying with each step that it's not too late. And with each step, her hope dies bit by bit.

A little voice in her head whispers, "*It's not the end of the world if they bring him in for questioning. They won't find anything and they'll have to let him go.*"

But she knows it's not that simple. She's overheard enough of her father's FBI stories to know that they don't just politely ask suspects questions and release them an hour later. They're not like cops. They'll keep him in custody for as long as it takes to get the answers they're looking for, especially if they have evidence. And Jareth doesn't have a lawyer, so there won't be anyone there to defend him and tell him what not to say.

And ultimately, even if they do let him go, her father will never let her see him again.

Not that that'll stop her.

Ring-ring! Ring-ring!

She flips open the phone immediately, before she can register that the number calling is not Jareth's.

"Hello?" she asks desperately.

"Veronica?" It's Jareth's voice! "It is you. I wasn't sure if I could trust the text."

"Jareth, the FBI is coming after you—" The words rush out without a breath between.

"I know," he says. "They tried to force me into a car, but I got away."

"Oh, thank god!" she exclaims, pressing her hand against her chest. "Where are you?"

"In a phone booth across from the diner," he says. "I didn't trust calling from my phone. They can probably track it, so I'm going to ditch it."

"Okay, stay right there! I'll catch a bus and be there as soon as I can. And Jareth?"

"I love you, too," he says. "See you soon."

Excitement forces its way through the bevy of emotions, spreading a brilliant smile across her face.

With new purpose, she closes the phone and heads to the nearest stop for the bus that will take her close to the diner.

The bus ride is agonizingly slow. Every time it stops to pick up a new passenger or let one off, the worry that Jareth will be found grows. Her leg doesn't stop bouncing until she reaches her destination: the post office a block north of the diner.

As soon as she gets off the bus, she makes a run for the

diner, sprinting down the sidewalk like her life depends on it. In a way, it does.

Jareth is her life.

The lights of the diner come into view at the end of the block, and Jareth is running toward her before she spots the phone booth across the street.

They collide in an embrace, locking their arms around each other like they haven't seen one another in years.

"You have no idea how happy I am to see you," she says into his thick black hair.

"No happier than I am to see you," he says, squeezing her waist even tighter.

When they finally pull away, they look into each other's eyes.

"What now?" she asks, her hands hanging around his neck.

"I'll find a place to hide," he says with a sigh, looking at her longingly as if he knows he'll soon have to let her go.

"Wherever you go, I'm coming with you," she asserts.

He shakes his head. "I can't ask you to do that. Your dad—"

She silences him with her finger to his lips. "I'm not going back home after the way he treated me. Taking away my phone like I was a spoiled child who deserved to lose a toy. Let him worry sick about the daughter he doesn't trust." That knowledge stings as she says the words, even though part of her knows she's earned his lack of trust.

Reluctance crashes like waves in Jareth's dark eyes as he looks down at her.

"So, where to?" she asks before he can mount any further objections.

He purses his lips, pondering. "Well, there is one place. It's a long shot, but it's the best idea I have."

Her thumb absently rubs the nape of his neck. She's so grateful to have him back in her arms. "Where?"

"The orphanage."

The night air is chilly, the late September breeze bringing in the fall season like a sneak thief, stealing what remained of summer's warmth.

Veronica rubs her arms as she hugs herself, having foolishly forgotten to grab a jacket in her haste to warn Jareth, and as they now wait outside the front door of Grace Orphanage, she greatly regrets the misstep.

At long last, the door opens, and Sister Agatha peers out, her graying hair still in its tight bun even though she's wrapped herself in a night robe ready for bed.

"Hello? Oh, Jareth?" Her face brightens as she recognizes him in the darkness. "What brings you here? And is that..." her eyes find Veronica, and recognition sparks anew. "Viv Styles? I didn't know you two were acquainted."

Jareth glances sidelong at Veronica with a look that begs the question, *"Viv Styles?"*

Veronica subtly rolls her eyes in an expression that says, *"I'll tell you later,"* then she nudges him forward with her elbow.

"Good evening, Sister," Jareth says, taking the lead. "Um, we actually need kind of a favor."

Sister Agatha doesn't miss their strange exchange, and her forehead wrinkles with a mixture of curiosity and concern. "Oh?"

Jareth steps forward, speaking in a hushed tone. "My friend, Viv"—he stresses the fake name—"has had a falling out with her family." He looks both ways clandestinely, and continues even more quietly, which makes Sister Agatha draw closer in intrigue. "She has...issues with her dad. She can't go back home, but she has nowhere else to go. And we can't stay at my house because that's the first place her dad will look. Is there any way you could find the grace in your heart to let us stay here for a few days?"

Sister Agatha's entire face becomes a map of wrinkles as she's about to argue, so Jareth adds, "At least until she can figure things out and find an alternative?"

The nun purses her lips, her discerning gray eyes passing back and forth between the two of them like some almighty righteous judge.

Veronica steps in, putting on her best puppy dog face. "Please, Sister, I promise we won't be a burden. We will help out in any way we can, earn our keep. We can care for the younger children. Anything, please." She cues the water works, constricting her voice. "I can't go back home—"

She only has to feign crying for a second before Sister Agatha rushes forward to hug her, rubbing her back and saying, "Oh child, of course, you can stay. Hush now. You're safe here."

"Thank you," Veronica sniffles, wiping her arm across her dry nose when they withdraw.

The sister holds Veronica at arm's length, her hands on both of Veronica's shoulders. "But, I must ask...are you with child?"

Veronica blushes as her eyes flick to Jareth, finding his cheeks just as red. "Oh, no." She shakes her head vehemently. "No, it's nothing like that. Jareth and I are saving ourselves until marriage." She reaches out for Jareth's hand and squeezes it, acting the part even though that ship has already sailed and sunk to the bottom of the ocean.

"Oh, good." Sister Agatha clasps her hands together. "Well, come on in. I'll find you both *separate* rooms."

Veronica and Jareth quietly snicker as she guides them inside.

She shows them to two rooms on opposite ends of a hall. When they get to the room Veronica will stay in, she says, "If you'll both be staying here, you'll have to abide by our rules. Lights out is at eight o'clock sharp. No fraternizing after that. No physical contact with the opposite sex—"

"I assure you, sister, we will be on our best behavior," Jareth pledges, and this makes Veronica frown internally. She's never been on her best behavior in her whole life.

Her warning voiced, Sister Agatha sits on the neatly made bed and pats it for Veronica to join her.

Veronica has no other choice but to oblige.

"I can't begin to know what hardships you're going through, but if you ever need to talk, I'm here for you," Sister Agatha says with such compassion that it makes Veronica feel guilty for lying to her. "Nuns are God's therapists, you know." She nods once as if to enforce the notion.

"Thank you, sister," Veronica says, forcing a hoarseness into her voice. "When I'm ready, I promise you'll be the first person I come to. I can't thank you enough for helping me—us—in our time of need."

Sister Agatha pats Veronica's hand on the bed. "All God's children need a little help now and then. That's what I was put on this earth for." She rises. "I'll let you two say your goodnights, then it's to bed with both of you." Then she heads out the door, giving them both the *eye* before leaving.

When her footsteps echo down the hall, Jareth comes in all the way and sits on the bed in the now empty spot. "So, *Viv*, I had no idea you and Sister Agatha were so close?" he accuses teasingly.

Veronica grimaces, hanging her head back as if to reject that she's been caught in a lie. "It was a few weeks ago when I had just started investigating Brielle and Tristan," she explains, exasperated. "I didn't even know you then."

Jareth chortles and nudges his elbow into her ribs, and they both laugh. "I guess it actually works to our benefit, her knowing you, or at least thinking she does." He gives her a look, and she rolls her eyes playfully. "Although, I bet you could get away with just about anything with those big brown eyes."

Veronica shrugs, feigning humility. "Well…" She smiles.

"We're safe here." He looks away, letting the weight of their circumstances sag his shoulders and facial features.

"Do you think they'll come looking for you here?" she can't help but ask.

He shakes his head without a moment of doubt. "No. My connection to this place is so far in the past, they'd have to be geniuses to come sniffing."

Veronica hangs her head to one side. "My dad is crazy clever."

He rests his head on her shoulder. "If they find us, we'll just keep running."

Veronica nods, though she's torn up inside. She hates that she's turned on her dad so irrefutably.

But she stands with Jareth. He's everything to her, and her dad is wrong.

She knows where her loyalties lie.

9

BRIELLE

Tristan is gone. Really gone.

And who knows when he's coming back.

She remains on the lawn for several minutes after he walks away, hugging her arms and letting the tears fall.

It's all her fault. If she hadn't kissed him, he wouldn't feel the need to run. He'd stick around and just lay low, like he told her to do.

Why can't he just do that? They could all agree to avoid the Gym for a while until things cool off. As long as they stay out of any more videos, the world will forget about the Super Suits eventually.

This isn't right. They're a team! Separating isn't the answer. What if something happens and they need him? What if Tristan gets in danger and needs them? He could get killed by Skins and they'd never know. It would've been a mistake for Jareth to leave weeks ago, when he thought he was protecting them.

And it's a mistake for Tristan to leave.

Brielle wipes her face and looks up, desperately searching the field for Tristan's silhouette. She can't let him go!

In the distance, the beams of his headlights flash, followed by the lazy grumble of his truck coming to life.

"No!" she hisses, sprinting across the field to catch him.

But he's already down the road before she even reaches the black top.

She swipes out her phone and calls him. It rings several times before it goes to voicemail. She calls again, and this time it goes straight to voicemail. He's clearly ignoring her.

"Dammit, Tristan," she grunts. "I'm not letting you leave!"

Spinning on her heel, she dashes to the carport where her bicycle is stored. She doesn't care that she's only dressed in a tank top and shorts, or that she'll have to ride without shoes. She's going to catch up to Tristan, even if she has to ride all the way to his house.

She digs her foot onto the pedal, the sudden turn of her back wheel kicking up clumps of dirt behind her, and she speeds across the lawn and down the road.

Even though Tristan keeps to the speed limit—thirty-five on this road—Brielle can only ride at a speed of fifteen miles an hour at best. She knows that, unless there happens to be a traffic jam, or a giant fissure opens up in the ground, she'll never catch up to him.

What if he doesn't go home? What if he was already packed and ready to leave wherever he planned to go? If she takes the route to his house, she could totally miss him!

She grits her teeth and cycles her feet even faster, ignoring the burning in her chest and throat, and the fact that she can hardly catch her breath.

As she crests over a hill, she sees a pair of red taillights up ahead. Relief washes over her for the briefest moment, until she notices the cluster of white, yellow and red lights around it.

What's going on?

She gets closer, but now with caution. Why is Tristan

parked out here? And why is there a vehicle parked sideways in front of him blocking the road? Some kind of random checkpoint or something? Her gut says otherwise.

"Hey, what the pitch!" Tristan yells, and she can now just make out that two men are yanking him out of his truck.

"Tristan!" she gasps, stomping on her pedals like her life depends on it. No, worse—Tristan's does!

She rams right into the guy farthest to the left, tucking in her head to roll on the ground as the impact throws her forward. She lands on her feet and jumps up, ready to pull the next guy off the boy she loves.

But Tristan is already on top of it. He must have used her sudden interruption to punch the other assailant, who is now flat on his back on the ground.

"Brielle? What are you doing here?" he demands, surprised but barely out of breath.

"I chased you to tell you not to leave," she pants, hands on her hips. "And it's a good thing I did. These Skins could have killed you, and none of us would have ever known what happened to you!"

"They're not Skins," he says, looking around at the two unconscious bodies on the ground and the large black Suburban parked sideways in front of him. "For one, they were way too easy to take out. And two, Skins don't usually attack like this, it's not their style." He points to the Suburban, which Brielle now realizes must have pulled out in front of Tristan and forced him to stop. Which means they were likely trying to grab him, not kill him.

Clutching her chest, she struggles to catch her breath. "If they're not Skins, who are they?"

"Judging by the black suits, black car and black guns, I'd say feds," he surmises.

The one she rammed with the bike groans and lifts his head. Tristan walks over and punches him in the jaw, which makes Brielle turn away. Somehow, knowing that these guys are only human makes the violence so much harder to handle. The guy is out cold again.

"Why would they do this?" she exclaims, chest tightening in renewed panic.

"My guess is that the truce with Jack is over, after the asteroid thing." Tristan sighs loudly and rakes his fingers over his hair, then begins to pace. "See, this is exactly why I have to leave. I can't lead the feds to the rest of you."

Before Brielle can object, Tristan's phone rings.

He checks it. "It's Jareth." He answers it.

Brielle waits, watching Tristan's face in the dim glow from the dome light flooding out the open door of his truck, and aching to tell him he can't go.

But as she watches, Tristan's face becomes more and more pinched, his eyes wider. "Hang on." He pulls the phone away from his ear and taps the speaker button, holding the phone out between them. "Okay, you're on speaker. Say that again."

"A couple of feds just tried to grab me near the house," says Jareth's voice through the phone. "I got away, but they're onto us, Tristan. They mentioned your name. We can't go back to HQ, there's no way they're not watching the house."

"Dammit," Tristan curses. "Yeah, they tried to get me, too, but luckily Brielle snuck up on them and helped me knock them out."

"Oh my god," Jareth groans.

"You're sure they only said my name?" Tristan inquires. "Not Brielle or Cassandra?"

"Nope, as far as I can tell, they only want you and me."

Tristan closes his eyes and nods, seeming relieved. "Where are you now?"

"At the orphanage with Veronica."

"Okay, good. Wait there for me. We'll get outta town—"

"No," Brielle asserts, crossing her arms.

"What? Brielle—" Tristan stammers, his tone argumentative.

"No, Tristan," she says with even more authority. "If there is one thing I know, it's that we can *not* split up. We all have to stay together, or at least within reach of one another. If you and Jareth go on the run, you might be safe from the feds —for a short while until they track you down again—but you'll both be more vulnerable to Skins."

Tristan lets out an exasperated scoff. "As of right now, the feds don't seem to be on to you and Cassandra, and I won't be responsible for putting you in even more danger. Besides, I have nowhere to go."

"You can come to my house," she blurts out.

"What?"

"Like you said, the feds aren't on to me." The more Tristan looks at her like she's insane, the more the argument forms in her head and becomes more and more convincing. "Even if they suspect, they don't have any evidence on me, not enough to bring me in. And if that changes, then we'll all leave together. We're a team, and that's how we're going to stay."

"She makes a good point," Jareth's voice interjects. Brielle can hear his own reluctance to leave, probably because of Veronica.

"You can't keep me in your room, your parents will definitely notice, and Frank is not going to let me stay," Tristan argues.

The idea hits like her bicycle hitting the fed. "The attic! Frank and Bea never go up there, and as long as you stay quiet, they'll never suspect."

Tristan's aversion visually dissolves, his expression looking more defeated than determined. "What about Jareth and Veronica?"

"Don't worry about us," Jareth responds. "We've got somewhere safe to bunker down for a little while."

Tristan chews on his bottom lip for a while as he considers all this. "Agh, fine. Call us soon as you can."

"Gotcha." Then the screen goes black, and Tristan shoves his phone back in his pocket.

Brielle can hardly contain the relief, victory and anticipation that's all but bursting in her chest right now.

Tristan picks up her bike and pulls it forward. "We'd better take off before they come to. For this plan to work, they can't see you. I'm pretty sure we knocked them out before they got a glimpse of you earlier. You really came out of nowhere."

He hands the bike to her, then heads to his open driver's side door. "Get home as quickly and quietly as you can. I'll be there soon."

Just like that, the jubilant swell in her chest deflates, replaced by the heavy weight of doubt. "Where are you going?"

"To ditch the truck somewhere, lead them away from your house so they won't have reason to look there," he says as he closes the door.

"Tristan, you are coming back, right?" she asks, gripping the edge of the rolled-down window.

His eyes meet hers, and there's not a single hint of deceit when he says, "I promise."

She smiles, then watches him drive out of sight before hopping on her bike and racing back home.

As she approaches, she rides up slowly, making sure there's no sign of feds around the house. When the coast looks clear, she sneaks back inside, grateful that all the lights are still off and that Frank and Bea didn't notice her missing.

She goes to her room and grabs a pillow and a couple blankets, then ventures out into the hall and up to the attic, which can only be reached by a pull-down ladder hidden in the ceiling of the laundry room. She climbs up and inspects the space. She's never been up here before, only ever having been informed of its existence during her first week living here.

The air is filled with dust, and every surface is covered with it, but like everything else in the house, the space is uncluttered and carefully organized. She spies the perfect opening beside the tiny circular window for Tristan to set up camp, so she lays out the blankets and pillow with care.

Her stomach twists into a tighter and tighter knot every time she reminds herself that she's going to be hiding Tristan here, in her house, right under Frank and Bea's nose. On the one hand, it's kind of thrilling in a teenage Romeo and Juliet sort of way. Well, if he hadn't rejected her a thousand times. But on the other hand, this is just one more secret that she's keeping from her parents.

But what other choice does she have? She refuses to let their team split up. And especially after rescuing Tristan tonight, knowing that he'll be where she can protect him is immensely comforting.

Once she has everything all set up, she goes back to her room to wait.

Hours have gone by since they parted ways. Tristan hadn't lied to her when he promised to come back. She would have sensed it. But what if he changed his mind? What if he decided to run after all? What if—

Knock, knock.

Her head immediately shoots to the window in the direction of the tapping, and her mental rambling goes completely silent when she sees Tristan's face through the glass.

Oh, thank pitch!

She quietly opens the window and helps him inside. "You came," she whispers.

"Of course," he whispers back, their eyes meeting again. "I made you a promise."

She smiles and throws her arms around his neck, his arms automatically closing around her back. The bare skin of his neck feels so good against her cheek. His hair smells so good. She gets lost in the feeling of him.

Suddenly, he pulls away, and she remembers herself.

"So... the attic?" he says, his eyes darting everywhere but on her.

"Right." She bites her lip and fights the burning in her cheeks. "This way."

She leads him to the laundry room and up the hidden stairs. She gestures to the makeshift bed she set for him in the back of the attic. "It's not the Four Seasons, but..."

"No, it's perfect," he says, looking at the blankets. "Thank you."

"No problem," she replies. "I'll try to check in tomorrow morning before Frank and Bea wake up. But if I can't, the house will be empty by eight, so you can come down after that for whatever you need."

"Okay. Thanks." He makes himself comfortable on the blankets.

She nods and heads for the stairs.

"Brielle?" His voice is soft and quiet, but she could hear it anywhere.

She looks back. "Yes?"

Even in the darkness, she can feel his eyes on her.

"Goodnight." His tone suggests he was about to say something else. But she lets it go.

"Goodnight." She descends the stairs and pushes them back into the ceiling, secure in the knowledge that, if nothing else, Tristan is safe. At least for now.

JACK

23:18

Jack slams his cell down on his desk, half-wishing the thing would smash. But it doesn't do what his world seems to be doing—implode.

He got away. Someone attacked us. We didn't get a good look.

The sheepish voice of his operative echoes through Jack's mind. Now Tristan is going to disappear like a puff of smoke. Just like Jareth did.

Just like Veronica has.

Not caring how useless it is, Jack leaves his home office and strides down the hallway. His stomach burns painfully as he reaches Veronica's door. He pushes it open, futilely hoping that her bedroom won't be achingly empty.

But it is. Like it has been since his daughter stormed out, her phone still in his hand. His little girl has run away.

Jack wipes a hand down his face, anger bubbling through the acid eating away at his stomach lining. Veronica's never been away this long, and he knows she doesn't intend on returning anytime soon.

All because of Ayers and the poisonous web he has her trapped in. Jack knows Jareth is involved somehow—there's no way it's a coincidence two orphans are living together and Veronica's boyfriend is clueless.

Brielle is the one he needs to make sure is more than just a hunch. And that girl, Cassandra.

Spinning on his heel, Jack returns to his desk. It hurts that he can't trust Veronica. It's killing him that he doesn't know where she is.

His only comfort right now is knowing that Veronica's tough. And stubborn. She's a survivor.

Picking his cell back up, Jack presses the familiar speed

dial. There's still one person he can trust. One person he can depend on to take these destructive aliens down.

It rings once before Logan picks up. "Hey, have you heard from her?"

Jack grimaces, hating that Logan is just as worried as he is. "No. Meet me at the FBI offices in twenty minutes."

It's time.

10

CASSANDRA

"Are you okay?" Brielle's voice is hushed on the other line. "Tristan told me what happened."

"Yeah, I'm okay." Cassandra looks around at her neighborhood outside the windows of her car, paranoid that something or someone might emerge from the shadows. "I just got home."

"Good." Brielle sighs. "With everything else that's happened tonight, I wanted to make sure the feds didn't come after you, too."

"Wait, what? Feds?" Cassandra's pulse spikes, like a dagger stabbing through her chest.

"Tristan almost got nabbed by a couple of them," Brielle explains in an even softer whisper. "Luckily I found him at just the right time and helped him get away. The same thing happened to Jareth near their house. He's gone into hiding with Veronica."

"Holy crap!" Cassandra hisses, sinking down in her seat as if to hide. "Should I do the same?"

"No. Jareth said the feds were only looking for him and Tristan. As far as we can tell, you and I aren't on their radar."

Cassandra's shoulders relax. "At least, not yet."

"For the time being, you and I just need to continue business as usual," Brielle says. "Go to school, stick to our routines, and avoid both the Gym and HQ. No using our powers unless we have to, no activating our suits."

Cassandra frowns. She hadn't gotten to really unwind at the Gym before she heard that gunshot and had to bail. Now she won't be able to rely on her powers as an emotional outlet. She'll have to go back to bottling it up. Great.

"So where are Jareth and Tristan going to hide? How will we know if they're okay?" she asks.

"Jareth and Veronica are at Grace Orphanage, so they're fine. And Tristan, well..." Cassandra can almost see Brielle biting her lip in that shy way of hers. "He's hiding out *in my attic*." The last three words are said so quietly they're like a hiss.

"No. Way!" Cassandra shouts, forgetting their circumstances for a moment and digging into this juicy gossip. "How is it that you two can go from kissing to not talking to each other to moving in together?"

"Pff, Cassie, it's not like that," Brielle retorts softly. "This is just the safest place for him to be right now."

"Aha, sure it is," Cassandra teases.

Brielle scoffs, and Cassandra giggles.

"Just keep me posted if you guys end up hooking up."

"Cassandra!" Brielle scolds, making Cassandra laugh even harder.

"Alright, you two have fun playing house. We'll catch up tomorrow."

"'Kay, bye." The call ends.

Cassandra looks at her house, reluctant that she has to go inside already. Although, at least she still has a house to come home to, unlike Jareth and Tristan. This is all her fault. If she hadn't been reckless, the FBI wouldn't be hunting them down like criminals.

Seriously, we saved the world. How about a thank you? She shakes her head, then gets out of the car and sluggishly treks to the front door.

"You're working late again?" her mother's voice shrills from the kitchen. "Well, when are you coming home? We've hardly seen you since the world didn't end!"

She must be talking to Cassandra's father.

Cassandra moves quietly into the kitchen to grab a protein shake from the fridge, and the fact that there's an open wine bottle on the counter and a half empty glass in her mother's hand doesn't escape her notice.

"Fine, I guess I'll see you then." Her mom hangs up the phone and looks at Cassandra. "Can you believe this? Your father is staying at the office again." She takes a swig of her red wine and shakes her head.

Cassandra closes the fridge and shrugs. "Well, money won't make itself." *Or steal itself from clients...*

"I guess. I just miss him." Her mother's botoxed face doesn't wrinkle, but Cassandra can tell that her words are genuine.

Cassandra is at a loss for words, because she doesn't miss him at all. "Well...maybe this time apart will be good for all of us. Maybe he'll come to appreciate the family he has."

Her mother's lips pout in what must be a frown. "You don't think he appreciates us?"

The familiar instinct to keep her opinions to herself tugs at Cassandra's insides. But that was the old Cassandra, she reminds herself. She doesn't have to live like that anymore.

"I just think he could be a little nicer, to both of us," she says.

Her mother scoffs. "He gives you everything. He spares no expense whenever you need something. A personal trainer for your track career, saving for your college education, that pretty little car you drive around. And whenever you need him, he's right there. Don't think I haven't noticed all the times he goes to your room in the evenings. It's like you two are best friends. Meanwhile, here I am, his wife, and he hardly ever even looks at me."

Cassandra's jaw falls open, and she's momentarily stunned into silence.

That's really what she thinks? That her husband is in their daughter's room to chat? That he's such a supportive father? She's actually jealous of the attention Cassandra gets?

She wouldn't be if she knew the nature of that attention.

"I mean, seriously, what more could you possibly want from him?" her mother jabs, rolling her eyes.

Warmth builds in Cassandra's palms before she can even register the anger writhing in her belly, and she reflexively digs her nails into their usual scars on her palms.

"Oh, I don't know, how about love?" Cassandra snaps without thinking. "You think I care about all the *stuff* he buys us? That's not love. When's the last time he actually showed you any true affection?"

Her mother narrows her eyes at Cassandra. "How can he when he's so busy doting on you?"

"You think he dotes on me?" All reigns on her temper have dissolved as years of repressed abuse rise to the surface, refusing to be caged. "If you want his so-called *attention*, you can have it! Maybe then you'd find out exactly the kind of man your husband is." She turns to storm out.

Her mom rounds the counter to block Cassandra's exit. "What is that supposed to mean?"

Cassandra had promised not to say anything to the authorities, but she never said she wouldn't tell her mother. And in that second, Cassandra decides it's time she knew.

"You know all those times he comes to my room at night?

Well, it's not to chat or bond. It's to punish me for whatever slight he's imagined I've committed against him."

The light in her mother's eyes dims even though her face doesn't move. "W-what are you talking about?" Her voice is a whole octave lower.

Cassandra scowls at her mother for a long moment, pages of words forming in her head of all the times her father has hounded her, cornered her, mutilated her. But finally, she knows no words would be enough.

She does a one-eighty and raises the back of her shirt, exposing her bare back. "*This* is what I'm talking about."

The gasp behind her is immediate and sharp.

Cassandra stays like that for a moment to let the image sink in, then lowers her shirt and slowly turns around. Her eyes sheepishly wander to her mother's face, hoping to find a fraction of the love and sympathy she so desperately needs in this moment.

Her mother's hands are cupped over her mouth, her eyes wide in shock. "How... How did you get those scars?" she asks hoarsely.

"How do you think?" Cassandra replies, her tone no longer attacking.

Her mom stares at her, and for a moment, Cassandra thinks that maybe she'll finally act like the mother she's supposed to be.

Then her mother shakes her head. "You—you're lying."

"What?" Cassandra exclaims.

"Your father wouldn't do something like this," her mother insists, head still obstinately shaking from side to side.

"W—b—you just saw the proof!" Cassandra stammers in disbelief. "How else could I have gotten these scars?"

"I don't know! Maybe they're not even real. Maybe you had them cosmetically applied before coming home, just to accuse your father, the man who's given you everything."

Cassandra is frozen in shock, her blood gone so cold that even the heat in her hands has extinguished. "You can't possibly believe that."

Her mother turns away from her, heading for the bottle of wine on the counter like this conversation never happened. "I think you need to go to your room, young lady."

Cassandra watches her mother with shock, outrage, and crushing disappointment.

There's nothing left to be said.

She flees the kitchen and goes to her room, not letting a single tear drop until she collapses against her closed door and sinks to the floor.

11

LOGAN

A lthough Logan's always been good at sensing others' emotions, it's obvious his father is tense as he leads him to the elevators in the FBI building the following day. A few people go to greet him only to quickly close their mouths and lower their hands, retracted thanks to Jack Cadbury's shuttered face.

Although the 'no-go' sign on Logan's father's forehead doesn't stop Flanagan from calling out.

"Cadbury, I need to see you in my office."

Logan's father stops beside the elevators. "Sure, give me thirty minutes."

Standing in line at the café, Flanagan hikes up his pants. "I meant now."

Logan glances at the five people in front of Flanagan, noting that he'll probably be at least fifteen minutes before he gets to his office himself. Although Logan keeps his face neutral, anger jabs hard in his gut. He's always sensed Flanagan's permanent state of low-level anxiety, but any sympathy died the moment Flanagan was promoted. Now, he's just an asshole with something to prove.

Logan's father indicates toward his son with his chin. "I'll be there in half an hour, Flanagan. I'm just seeing Logan off."

Flanagan frowns, his eyes darting to the people around him. "Sure, you go see your adult son off," he mutters loud enough for Logan and his father to hear. "Make sure you hold his hand in the parking lot…"

His father's flash of annoyance is bright but brief. "See you upstairs in thirty."

The elevator dings and the doors slide open. They step in and his father presses the button for the lowest parking lot floor. Logan decides against pointing out that his car is on the second floor below ground. It'll give him time to talk about more important stuff.

He jams his clenched hands in his pockets. "I can't believe that douche is your boss."

His father's gaze flickers his way before turning back to the flashing buttons as they descend. "Flanagan always knew how to kiss ass."

Unlike Logan's dad. Instead, he developed a set of theories that no one wanted to hear. Beliefs that others ridiculed him for.

And then the Super Suits appeared.

Logan takes a certain sense of satisfaction in knowing he supported and believed his father long before anyone else thought to pay attention to him. Veronica needs to learn that sort of loyalty.

"I don't know how you stop yourself from punching that brown-nosing face of his," he mutters.

His father's lips twitch. "I realized it doesn't matter anymore."

About to ask what he means by that, Logan pauses when he notes that the elevator has reached the lowest level…and is still moving. He freezes, mentally scanning his father's reaction. All he picks up is a quiet sense of satisfaction. And a slow fizzing sense of anticipation.

His father isn't worried. In fact, he's looking forward to whatever's about to happen.

The elevator slows to a stop and Logan holds his breath as the doors slide open. All that greets him are a set of frosted glass doors, cement-lined corridors leading both left and right.

Logan follows his father as he steps out, unsure what he's feeling. Nervous. Excited. Like he's standing on a precipice.

His father pauses as the lift doors close, glancing over his shoulder. "Logan, I've been wanting to show you this for quite a while now."

So many questions are clamoring for answers. Show him what? Where are they? Who else knows this is here? What the hell is going on?

His father swipes the back of his hand over a sensor pad beside the door and they *whoosh* open. "Welcome to Nebula, son."

Logan's left speechless as they enter a large room. Several rows of computers stretch left and right, a central walkway leading down the middle. About a dozen people are there, most sitting before a computer, one or two standing as they scribble on a clipboard. Several look up, nodding differentialy at Logan's father before returning to their work. No one seems to take much notice of the large screen along the back wall that's projecting a crystal clear image of star-spangled space.

"Nebula?" Logan chokes, unsure what he's supposed to make of all this.

His father nods. "Our mission is to protect Earth from extraterrestrial threats. We're funded by the UN and are a secret cache of the US government, although we have international jurisdiction." His eyes glint as he smiles. "We operate as a sub-branch of the FBI."

Blinking, Logan tries to process all the information, one fact jumping out at him the most. His father said 'we.' The fierce pride he senses only reinforces the word.

"You're a part of this? Of Nebula?"

His father's smile stretches to a grin. "Let me show you something else."

He leads Logan out of the tech-saturated room. In the corridor, his father turns left but quickly stops at a door on the other side of the concrete hall. Once again, he swipes the back of his hand over a sensor and the door slides open.

Logan finds himself in an office, albeit an impressive one. Thick blue carpet lines the floor, with a large timber desk at the back, leather chairs on either side. Although there are no windows, the room is brightly lit, the American flag proudly standing in the two back corners, what looks like a door tucked behind each one.

"Wow," Logan says. He almost feels like he's in the White House, standing in the Presidential office.

His father indicates for Logan to take the seat in front of the massive, ornate desk as he moves around and sits on the other side.

Logan's brows spike up. "This is your desk?"

His father sits down and clasps his hands on the smooth timber surface. "I'm the director of Nebula, Logan."

Logan flops into the plush chair, mind reeling. No wonder Flanagan doesn't get to his father anymore. He outranks him thousandfold.

"Nebula is a top secret organization," his father says gravely. "Only a handful of the world's leaders know we exist." His eyes blaze. "And I'd like you to join us."

Logan's lost the ability to move. He doesn't blink. His

lungs are frozen mid breath. His whole body is in suspended animation.

His father trusted him enough to bring him into the FBI. Not only that, into an organization that exists outside of mainstream knowledge.

Everything he's ever wanted is being handed to him in this moment.

Logan leans forward. "Where do I sign up?"

His father's burst of joy almost rivals the sweet, soaring happiness that's exploding through Logan. "I was hoping you'd say that."

"Dad…" Logan clears his throat. "I won't let you down."

"You never have, son. That's why you're here. You had a taste of what we're up against with the man you captured. This fight needs good men like you."

Logan's not sure how he's not levitating, he's so freaking happy. He grips the arms of the chair, physically anchoring himself as he gets his head in the game. Determination solidifies around him, forming an unshakeable foundation.

He'll always make this man proud. He'll do whatever it takes to prove Jack Cadbury is the hero he's always known he is.

Logan's gaze connects with his father. "What's the brief?"

Although his father's face becomes all business, Logan can still sense the quiet warmth that's lodged in his chest. "The Super Suits showing up just proved what we've suspected—things are happening out there."

And when his father says "out there", he means beyond the layers of Earth's atmosphere.

His father picks up a remote and presses a button. A large screen on the right that Logan hadn't noticed flickers to life, showing the same image of space that was on in the room full of computers.

"Is that where it happened? Where the Super Suits destroyed the asteroid?"

"This is where we've traced the first appearance of the asteroid." His father's lips thin. "It essentially came out of nowhere."

Logan shakes his head. "But that's not possible."

"Our best guess is a singularity has been created in that location."

"Created?"

"There's no way to tell—we don't have the technology to 'see' black holes yet. And yes, we believe it was created. Singularities are made either when a star collapses, creating a supernova, which hasn't happened. Or has existed since the galaxy was formed, which is also not the case. And if this singularity was created, it quite possibly has another side, which would make it a wormhole."

"But that means…"

"We're dealing with some pretty advanced technology."

Alien technology.

Alien technology that has created a black hole.

Logan peers more closely at the image, but it may as well be a photo. Nothing moves on the screen. "What's it doing?"

"Nothing, as far as we can tell." His father's gaze sharpens. "For the moment."

For the first time, Logan realizes what they're up against. What else could come through the wormhole?

What already has…

His jaw tightens. "What do I need to do?"

"We need to find out who or what this Chardis is. Who or what the Super Suits are. We need to find out how we stop this." His clasped hands tighten. "And Tristan Ayers has been the one consistent link in all of this."

Nodding curtly, Logan shifts to the edge of his seat. "What do we know?"

"That he's probably part of some secret organization himself. That his adoptive parents died fighting to keep their mission a secret. That the words Zodiac Guardians means something to them."

Logan nods again, carefully cataloguing the information.

His father's nostrils flare as he draws in a breath. "And that he's probably recruiting people to his cause."

Just like Nebula, whatever evil they're planning would need people to fight.

Logan's gaze snaps to his father's. "You don't think Veronica..."

His father looks away. "Jareth Stone is believed to be linked, somehow."

Veronica's boyfriend.

"I'd like to think that Veronica is smarter than that," his father says quietly.

Except Logan's sister isn't here, in their father's office, learning about the existence of Nebula.

Veronica's potential betrayal only solidifies Logan's determination. It seems loyalty runs deeper than blood ties do.

"We suspect Brielle Pierce is, too. We don't have enough on her, yet, but we sent agents to apprehend Ayers and Stone." Jack's hands tighten. "They both escaped and I suspect they're going to drop off the radar."

His gaze settles unflinchingly on his father. "What do you want me to do?"

"We need to keep an eye on anyone associated with Ayers." His father's eyes turn piercing. "Get close so we can learn what we need to."

Logan pushes to his feet, powered by a powerful sense of purpose. "Yes, sir. I'll get on it straight away."

His father stands, too. "I have no doubt you're going to be

an asset to this organization, son. To the fight against this deadly alien threat."

"You know I'll do everything I can to protect Earth."

His father straightens, his chest expanding. "Welcome to Nebula, Logan."

Logan wants to salute his father. Or hug him. Or jump into his arms like he did when he was a kid.

Instead, he nods once. The short, sharp movement is a promise. A vow. An oath to the man who taught him what love and loyalty is.

And Logan knows exactly where to start.

The beautiful blonde girl will be his first mark.

12

TRISTAN

Tristan can't stay here.

For one, he can barely squeeze his shoulders through the single, small round window up here, and Zarius always told him to make sure he has more than one escape route. If the feds or Skins come looking, Tristan needs a way out.

Two, he's been here a day and he already feels like a caged animal. Although the attic is spacious enough, it feels like it's shrinking every hour. The quick recon he did after everyone left wasn't enough to stem the cabin fever that's slowly setting in.

He'd woken after a fitful night's sleep, listening to the Pierce family moving about the house. He couldn't make out any words, but the muffled voices had created a soothing rhythm as they ate breakfast and prepared for the day.

A pang of grief had gripped Tristan's chest as he remembered mornings when he had a family, too. Tess in the kitchen. Zarius hovering around, not because he had any idea how to cook, just because he liked to be near her.

Tristan had wanted to pace—ideally go for a run—to burn

off the tension that never seems far away. It's forever knotting his muscles, tangling his mind. But he couldn't. He can't afford to make any noise.

A text had arrived then, as if Brielle could sense his downward spiral.

There's a care package in my room. See you after school.

The house had fallen quiet not long later. Tristan waited for a good half an hour before tiptoeing down. Somehow, he'd found Brielle's room following nothing but instinct. Her room is just what he thought it would be—neat, orderly, a handful of framed photos of her and the Pierces already scattered around.

His care package was on the bed, wrapped in a towel. He'd sat down, opening it like a gift.

Inside were some toiletries. Food and bottled water. A cell phone charger. A few choc-chip cookies wrapped in foil. Of course, Brielle had thought of everything.

But…that's the problem. He's here, being reminded of her thoughtfulness and delicious cooking. He was supposed to be putting distance between them.

Tristan tamps down on the urge to pace again. His quick foray around the house so he could get a sense of the layout and his brief shower had been all he afforded himself before he returned to the attic. All it would take is Frank or Bea coming home unexpectedly because they forgot something and Tristan could be discovered. The last thing he wants to do is cause issues for Brielle with her adoptive parents. The happy chatter from this morning had been evidence of how well things are going for them.

Plus, pacing won't solve his problem.

Not unless he paces the hell out of here.

Except Jareth and Veronica are now laying low, too. And Cassandra is going back to normality, as if she never destroyed a planetoid with her bare hands. The best thing

Tristan can do is disappear for a while, which is exactly what he was planning on doing.

Just not in the same house as the one girl he can't stay away from.

He rakes his fingers through his hair. The kiss changed everything, and not for the better.

And yet, those moments are like a blinding star in his memory. Bright. Breathtaking. Beautiful.

The sound of a door opening and closing has him pausing. Although he can't hear anything, he senses it's Brielle. Something in his chest just sparked.

A few moments pass and the ladder drops down, sending eddies of dust scooting over the wooden floor. Brielle appears a moment later, climbing into the attic then stopping beside the opening.

"Hey," she says quietly.

Tristan's first urge is to go to her. It always is. But he locks his knees, telling his feet to grow roots. "Hey. How was school?"

Brielle shrugs. "Same old, same old. A whole lot quieter without you or Jareth."

The words tug at Tristan's chest. Brielle was a loner before the other Zodiacs came along. Just like the rest of them, she knew she was different, but she assumed that made her an outsider.

"And Cassandra?" he asks.

"She spent the day with Suki and Jen."

Tristan nods. That's what Cassandra's supposed to be doing. But it still leaves Brielle alone...

He straightens his spine. He was going to leave her, anyway, which means today would've been no different. He just couldn't think of how else they can move forward.

Brielle takes a small step toward him. "Is there anything

else you need? I know it must be hard for you to be stuck up here."

Although, he probably has it easier than Brielle right now. "A laptop would be good. So I can get a sense of what's going on out there."

She nods, chewing on her lip. "I'm sure we have a spare. I'll leave it under the bed."

"Thanks."

"And are you okay for...you know..." Her cheeks flush bright pink as she waves a hand in his general direction.

Tristan chuckles as he realizes what she's talking about. He glances at the window that's just large enough for him to squeeze through. "I'll duck outside if things get urgent."

Brielle nods, looking relieved that it's sorted. "Bea will be home shortly. We usually cook dinner together."

A mixture of relief and disappointment that she'll be leaving so soon tumbles through Tristan. "Sounds fun. Plus, I'm sure you've got homework to do."

She nods once more, back to chewing her lip. The awkwardness that had been hovering between them gains life in the silence that stretches out, thickening the air. Tristan's hands compulsively clench and unclench. He wills Brielle to go.

He wishes she could stay.

Brielle looks up, resoluteness stamping across her features. She takes another step into the attic, shrinking the space between them. "I had an idea today."

There's something in her tone that has Tristan stilling. Why does he get the sense she's not talking about feds or Skins or a new recipe for caramel mud cake?

"Yeah?"

"We can't keep going like this, Tristan. It's not good for the Zodiacs." Her moss green gaze settles on his. "Or for either of us."

His gut clenches. "I know. I'm the one who tried to leave, remember?"

She shakes her head, the dark strands of her hair brushing her cheeks. "That wasn't the solution. The Zodiacs need to stay together."

Tristan snaps his mouth shut, acknowledging she's right. On all accounts. He sighs. "What's your idea?"

Another step and there are only a few feet between them. It means Tristan can see the way Brielle draws in a fortifying breath.

"We're drawn to each other, Tristan. Whether it's right or wrong, neither of us can deny that."

Tristan nods, his throat tight. The time-stopping, heart-soaring, foundation-rocking kiss was proof of that.

"And staying apart isn't working." Her cheeks flush a delicate pink, but her gaze doesn't leave his. "The way I see it, why not give it—us—a chance?"

"But—"

Her hand comes up to stop him. "I know about the Gemini soulmate. I'm not talking about exchanging promise rings, Tristan. I'm talking about being together, no strings attached."

Tristan blinks. *Be together?* "But...how?"

Her lips tip up in a soft smile. "It doesn't have to be that hard. Or complicated. Why not just keep things casual? See what that looks like?"

Images spiral through Tristan's mind. The two of them holding hands. Losing the strain of hiding how he feels for her. Making Brielle laugh instead of frown, for a change.

His gaze flickers to her lips. Kissing again. And again. And again.

He clears his throat, realizing he just took a step forward. "Are you okay with that?"

If his Gemini soulmate turns up, everything would change.

Brielle's eyes are luminous as she nods. "I really am. We have no idea what's ahead of us. Why fight this, too?"

A new feeling is bubbling up through Tristan. One he's not sure he's felt before. It's warm and light and delicious. "You only live once kinda of thing?"

"We're Zodiacs, we've learned that more than anyone."

She's right. Most of them have lost someone they cared about in the battle against Chardis.

Brielle seems to be holding her breath. How much courage did it take for her to propose this? When all Tristan has done is push her away?

His gaze roams her face, taking in the sweet pink of her cheeks, her parted mouth as she waits. Her glorious green eyes are full of everything he's feeling.

Nervousness.

Anticipation.

The thrill of being on a precipice.

"Where do I sign up?" he asks softly. Excitedly.

Brielle angles her chin up, the light bathing lips. "Right here," she breathes.

Tristan lets go of the final threads of his fragile self-control and draws her to him. Gently, eagerly, they curve into each other, glorying in all the ways they fit. Everything within Tristan calms and soars all at once.

Without conscious thought, his head tips toward hers, but he pauses, hovering as he breathes in her familiar scent. This isn't the impulsive moment they shared on the rooftop. A stolen, rushed kiss where he'll have to pull away after.

This is a kiss that can take as long as it likes.

Tristan's hands come up to cup Brielle's face, his thumbs caressing her cheekbones. Her eyes flutter closed, bliss lighting her beautiful features. Bliss that Tristan put there.

His chest expands, wanting to treasure this moment indefinitely.

Except, it's not enough. He wants to taste her. Needs to give her more.

He brushes his lips against hers in a heated graze. Brielle's breath stutters and her hands come up to grasp his. Heat coils around them, spiking their desire.

With a groan, Tristan's mouth covers hers. Their lips mold and meld, their bodies press closer together. Brielle's hands slip around his neck, her fingers tickling his hair and sending heavenly shivers down his spine.

Tongues delve and explore and taste. Tristan can't seem to get enough, but then again, neither can Brielle. Her fingers hungrily clutch at his hair, pulling him even closer. His arms band around her, compressing the desire between their quivering bodies.

"Brielle? Are you home?"

Although Bea's voice is faint, it's enough for the two of them to draw apart with a start. Panting and flushed, they smile at each other.

"I need to get down there before she comes looking," Brielle murmurs, regret evident in her tone.

"You really do," Tristan agrees, although he doesn't release her.

A quick brush of her lips and Brielle pulls back. She rushes toward the ladder, glancing over her shoulder as she's about to descend. A sweet smile dances over her kiss-moistened lips. "I'll see you tomorrow."

Her words are so full of promise, Tristan's heart compulsively happy dances.

He grins. "I'll be here."

Waiting.

For once, looking forward to—no, impatiently waiting—for what the next day will bring.

13

BRIELLE

The same shapes that usually form themselves in the popcorn ceiling above Brielle's bed appear this morning, but as she stares up at them, all she can see is Tristan.

Her cheeks haven't stopped burning since last night. His kisses still tingle on her lips. And his delicious scent is all over her hands.

Knowing that he's up there was enough to quicken her pulse before, but now the beautiful knowledge that the only barriers between them are the attic rafters and the thin drywall of her ceiling have her heart threatening to burst from her chest and bounce around the room.

Today is Saturday. How is she going to be able to stand an entire day in this house with her parents knowing she can't steal away to be with the guy of her dreams who's waiting just a few feet above her head?

And how is she going to be able to face her parents knowing she's keeping this giant secret right under their noses?

Hiding Tristan in her attic may not technically be a lie—she never said anything on the subject to them—but it makes her feel guilty all the same. It's the most dishonest thing she's ever done.

And she'd do it over and over again. What wouldn't she do for Tristan?

Knock, knock.

Brielle shoots up in bed, her cheeks on fire and a lump lodged in her throat—as if just thinking of her treachery were a crime.

The door slowly cracks open and Bea peers inside. "Good morning. You awake?"

Brielle's heart thuds against her ribcage. Bea doesn't usually come into her room like this on Saturday mornings. Or any morning, for that matter. Could she have found Tristan?

No, if she had, Brielle didn't think she would have bothered knocking.

"Yep." Brielle stretches and feigns a yawn. "What's up?"

Bea opens the door more fully and steps into the doorway. "Frank and I have to go into the city for a grocery run. Costco is supposed to have a new shipment of toilet paper, and we're hoping to get there before they sell out again—can you believe how crazy people get when there's any kind of scare?" She throws her hands up and laughs. "Anyway, did you wanna come with us?"

Bea and Frank are leaving the house. A grocery trip to the city will take them most of the day.

And they're giving her the option to stay home.

She struggles to contain her excitement and eagerness as she shakes her head and says, "Nah, I think I'll stay in today."

"You sure?" Bea asks, the tilting of her head making a lock of dark brown hair fall over her shoulder. "You won't be bored being here all by yourself?"

Brielle's heart drops to the bottom of her stomach. "Nope, I'll be fine."

"Okay. We're planning to go out to dinner. Want us to bring you something back?" Bea offers, her hand on the doorknob ready to retreat.

"Don't worry about me," Brielle says, hoping she doesn't look as sneaky as she feels. "You guys take your time. I don't think you two have had a night out by yourselves since I moved in."

Bea's brow flares. "Oh my goodness, you're right! I think we will do just that. Thanks for the suggestion!"

Brielle just smiles as Bea closes the door, then she flops down onto her pillow, and the smile blossoms from ear to ear.

She's going to have Tristan all to herself, in her house, *all day!*

Filled with fresh excitement, she hops out of bed and enjoys a quick breakfast with Frank and Bea before they leave. Brielle can hardly concentrate on chewing her bacon as she watches them eat, her leg bouncing impatiently.

When they finally leave, Brielle rushes to her room to make herself presentable. She rummages through her wardrobe again and again. This is the longest it's taken her to pick an outfit since her first meeting with her parents. Eventually, she decides on a lacey pink blouse and jean shorts. Then she brushes her hair and teeth and even puts on a bit of mascara.

The girl looking back at her in the mirror is really quite pretty, and happier than she's ever seen her reflection before. It's almost like she's seeing herself for the first time. The version of herself that belongs to Tristan.

She puts together a breakfast tray and carries it on top of a spare laptop to the attic stairs. Her feet wobble as they ascend the steps, and she's surprised—and relieved—she doesn't trip before she makes it to the top.

Tristan is sitting near the window, his eyes locked on her

as she emerges from the floor entrance. His hair is handsomely tousled, and she can't help but bite her lip as she imagines combing her fingers through it.

"Good morning," she greets softly. "I brought you some breakfast, and a laptop, as promised."

Tristan comes forward and reaches out to accept her offerings. "Here, let me get those for you." He takes the tray and laptop and sets them on the floor beside his makeshift bed. "I heard Frank's car leave and I assumed you went with him."

Her cheeks tangibly redden as she prepares what she has to say. "Actually, Frank and Bea went to the city for a grocery run. They'll be gone most of the day. They offered for me to go with them, but I had other things in mind."

He takes a step closer, his blue eyes blazing brightly in the dim attic. "Oh? Like what?" His hands slowly reach out and land on her hips, pulling her closer. The feel of his fingertips grazing her skin above her shorts is almost enough to make her knees buckle.

She rests her hands on his chest, savoring how firm it feels under the fabric of his T-shirt. His face is close enough that she can feel his breath on her face, and it's filled with the familiar sweet scent of him. His lips part, and suddenly they have her mesmerized. Her heart is beating so fast, it's like a buzzing in her chest.

She sucks in a breath. "Your breakfast is going to get cold," she squeaks out.

"Let it," he says, and suddenly those pink lips she hasn't stopped thinking about all night are on hers.

His hands slide from her hips to her lower back, pressing as they move to crush her against him. She gasps, parting her lips, and Tristan's hungry tongue eagerly accepts the accidental invitation. The caress of his tongue against hers is utter bliss, radiating euphoria throughout her body.

Together, they fall into a trance. Their mouths move in perfect rhythm with one another, opening and closing, exploring and tasting in a flawless and delicious dance. His fingertips continue to rub back and forth at the skin of her lower back just over her pant-line, the sensation driving her further into madness. She's not sure how they got there, but when they finally break for air, she finds herself on top of Tristan on the floor, his blankets tangled around them.

They stare into each other's eyes for a moment, and his are half-lidded and hazy, his lips puffy and impossibly tempting.

He swallows. "So, is this what you had in mind for today?" he murmurs, unable to break his gaze away from her lips.

A nervous giggle trips up her throat, and she bashfully climbs off of him, perching next to him. "I was thinking more along the lines of us spending time together, but…" She bites her lower lip. "Kissing works."

He props himself up on his left elbow and angles toward her. "I could honestly kiss you all day."

Her cheeks burn, and she can't help but turn away to hide the shy smile.

"But, I need some personal time," he admits with an awkward laugh.

"Oh, of course," Brielle blurts. After being cooped up all night in a cramped attic, anyone would.

"After that, how about we stay downstairs?" he suggests. "Anything has got to be more comfortable than this." He pats the blankets that barely cushion him from the hardwood floor.

"Sure. We can watch Netflix in my room?" Somehow, the thought of being alone with Tristan in her room is even more thrilling than being alone with him in the attic.

"Sounds perfect," he says with a grin. He sits up and pecks

her cheek before climbing to his feet, grabbing the breakfast tray, and heading down the stairs.

She follows shortly after and skips to her room. Only then does she notice how messy it is. Her bed is disheveled, there are various items of clothing scattered all over the floor, and her desk looks like a paper bomb exploded.

Unsure of how much time Tristan will need, she immediately begins gathering the clothes off the floor, balling them up against her chest as fast as she can. She dumps the armload into the bin in her closet, slides the door closed, then rushes to tidy up her desk, shuffling the papers into one neat stack. Lastly, she dashes over to her bed to smooth out the sheets and comforter.

Just as she tucks the edge of the comforter under her pillow, she hears footsteps approaching down the hall. She hops onto her bed and crosses her legs under her, trying to look casual, as if she'd just been sitting here waiting for him.

Tristan appears in the doorway, and looking surprisingly shy, hovers against the frame. The slight pink to his cheeks only makes him more adorable, and suddenly the distance between them feels too large and uncomfortable.

As if he feels it too, he pushes away from the doorframe and moves closer, like he's being pulled by an invisible force. The same one that has her leaning in his direction.

He sits on her bed, his thigh brushing against her knee. "So, what should we watch?"

Brielle pulls her laptop off her bedside table and opens it in her lap. "Since you're the captive here, why don't you pick?"

"I wouldn't exactly say I'm an unwilling prisoner," he says, winking at her. "Lady's choice."

She giggles. "Okay."

She chooses the latest Netflix produced comedy and clicks play, then sets the laptop on the edge of her bedside table, angling the screen for the best picture. The whole time, she's very aware of the way Tristan's eyes follow her every movement, and she just knows that he wants the same thing as she does.

Without a word between them, Brielle stretches out on her bed and rolls to her side facing the screen, and Tristan follows suit behind her, putting one arm around her and using the other to prop his head just above hers. They fit so perfectly, and Brielle can't help but close her eyes to savor the feel of his body against hers.

The movie plays, and she's sure it would have been a hilarious movie, if she could concentrate on a single minute of it. Tristan's free hand traces gently up and down her bare arm, trailing sizzling electricity and sending out shock waves that make it impossible to focus on anything else.

Halfway through the movie, they're kissing again, and they don't stop until they realize the room has gone silent because the movie ended. Tristan taps another movie, and the cycle starts all over again.

They spend the day like this, until the afternoon sun sneaking through her curtains reminds her that neither of them has eaten lunch and it's almost dinner time.

"Let me make you dinner," she suggests, her lips tired and a bit chapped, but in the best way.

"Only if I get to help," he responds.

"Well then that limits us to spaghetti or sandwiches," she teases, sliding off the bed.

He frowns at her playfully. "Low blow, Bri. Low blow."

She laughs and leads him to the kitchen, proceeding to close every blind lest wandering eyes see Tristan.

She pulls out a pot from one of the lower cabinets and fills it up with water from the faucet. As she places it on the large burner on the stove, Tristan opens a box of spaghetti from the pantry, ready to pour it in.

Grabbing his wrist, she stops him. "The water has to be boiling first," she informs, chuckling under her breath. "You really don't have any kitchen skills, do you?"

"On the contrary." He leans against the counter and crosses his arms. "I have the most important culinary skill of all."

"Oh yeah, what would that be?" she asks with a skeptical brow inclined.

He shrugs. "Eating, of course. I'm actually quite the expert at that."

Brielle shakes her head and laughs, then gets a roll from the pantry, a garlic butter from the fridge and a bread knife and sets them on the counter next to Tristan. "Here's something I know you can do. Slice the bread and butter it, then set it on this tray"—she hands him a cookie sheet—"to toast in the oven."

"Can do," Tristan says, then gets to work on the garlic bread.

He cuts and spreads while she stirs the marinara sauce and waits for the water in the other pot to boil. As soon as the cookie sheet is filled, she sets the oven to broil and he slides the tray inside. She sets the timer, and when it goes off, he removes the bread and turns the oven off.

It suddenly hits Brielle that they do all this without saying a word. Not because they're uncomfortable, but because they don't need to. Tristan does what she needs without her having to say it. Have they always worked this well together? They just...fit.

When the food is all done, they set the table together, and again Tristan seems to know what to do before she can ask.

They sit and begin to eat, enjoying the fruits of their joint labor.

"You didn't even burn the bread," she teases, holding one up in preparation to take a bite.

"See, I'm not completely useless in the kitchen," he says, piling spaghetti onto his own garlic toast with his fork.

"What are you doing?" she asks, watching with amused curiosity.

"Making a spaghetti sandwich," he replies, as if it's obvious. Then he folds the toast around the pile of noodles and lifts it to his mouth. "Don't knock it till you try it." He opens his mouth wide and takes a big bite.

"Hmm," she hums skeptically, then decides to try it his way anyway. She scoops an extra saucy bundle of spaghetti onto her bread, folds it, and bites into it. The crunch of the bread pairs surprisingly well with the soft noodles and the tangy sauce. "Mm!"

"See, told ya," he says with a mouthful.

Suddenly, light flashes through the closed blinds of the kitchen door, followed soon after by the sound of doors closing.

Frank and Bea are home!

Tristan automatically grabs his plate and runs down the hall. He tramples up the steps hastily, racing Frank and Bea to the door.

"Sorry," Brielle mouths before she pushes the staircase back up into the ceiling.

The kitchen door opens just as Brielle hurries back into the kitchen, heart pounding.

"Hey, did you guys have a good time?" she asks, her pitch a little too high.

Bea takes her purse off her shoulder and hangs it on the rack. "We had the best dinner. Thanks so much for giving us the green light to go out."

"Of course! You guys deserve it." *That and so much more...*

"What did you get up to today?" Frank asks, moving to the fridge. "Smells like something good."

"Oh, just...watched some TV," Brielle summarizes

vaguely. It's not a lie. She and Tristan did at least attempt to watch some things.

"This is a lot of spaghetti for just you," he notices, peering into the pot on the stove.

She swallows. "You guys are welcome to have some if you like. I definitely can't eat it all."

"No thanks, I'm beyond full," Bea says, waving one hand and covering her belly with the other. "Would you mind helping me bring in some groceries?"

"Absolutely," Brielle says and follows her into the garage.

Brielle helps Bea and Frank bring in all the groceries and put them away, the whole time thinking about just how close she came to getting caught.

But it was worth it. Today was the best day of her life.

Maybe this could really work. Maybe she and Tristan could really be happy together. At least for a little while.

And she's going to hang onto him as long as she possibly can.

14

CASSANDRA

"The black suit is dope," Zayn says around a mouthful of vanilla fro-yo.

"No way, the pink suit is way cooler," Suki argues, holding her spoon up between bites.

Zayn frowns and shakes his head. "You just think that because it clearly has a chick in it. She didn't even do anything. She was just floating on the sidelines while the gold chick did all the work."

"Well, so were the two guys." Suki points her still-full spoon at Zayn accusingly. "You just like the black one because the purple one isn't *manly* enough for you." She bobs her head sarcastically as she says the word "manly." "If you ask me, the dude in the purple suit is the coolest one of all. Gotta have a real pair of balls to fly around in that color."

Cassandra chokes on the strawberry she'd been trying to swallow before Suki's unknowing comment about what may or may not be in Tristan's pants got in the way.

She stands up and mumbles, "I'm going to the little girls' room," then stomps off back into Creamy Dreams, leaving the two to continue arguing about the same stupid topic.

Honestly, Cassandra's heard enough of it for a lifetime. Both the talk of the Super Suits, and Suki and Zayn's arguing. They've been doing that non-stop lately, ever since they both started hanging out together after their break-up. Seriously, they need to just get a room already. Get back together, which they both clearly want, and spare Cassandra from having to listen to them.

On that note, so should Brielle and Tristan. Before they went off the grid, their awkward silence was almost as bad as Zayn and Suki's bickering. She hopes their forced confinement has led to something. Oh great, now she's thinking about Tristan's balls again. Dammit!

Smack!

"Oops, I'm so sorry!" the guy apologizes before she can even process that they bumped shoulders.

She rubs her increasingly sore shoulder and looks up, ready to chew the guy out.

Whoa...

"No, totally my fault, I wasn't paying attention to where I was going," she says with a playful wave of her hand, flaunting a demure smile.

Mr. Tall Dark and Handsome returns it with a set of flawless pearly whites of his own, his chocolate brown eyes twinkling as they unabashedly scan her figure. "No worries. You can bump into me any time."

Cassandra giggles flirtatiously, then holds out her hand. "I'm Cassandra."

He accepts it, his hand warm and strong as it wraps around hers, and the touch sends an electric tingle up her arm. "Logan."

"I've never seen you here before, Logan," she says, savoring his touch as their hands slowly fall away from each other.

"Really? Because I've seen you." The way he says it makes

her cheeks instantly hot. "Don't you normally hang out with two guys and two other girls?"

She arches a brow and lifts one side of her glossed lips in a smirk. "So...bumping into me wasn't an accident, after all?"

He laughs and shoves his hands in the front pockets of his jeans, shrugging as he does so. "Maybe. Maybe not."

Her smile widens, and suddenly she doesn't know what to do with her hands. Should she cross them under her chest? Hook her thumbs onto her belt loops? She moves her hands to her hips only to realize there are no belt loops. Because she's wearing yoga pants. Omigod, she must look like a weirdo, rubbing her hips like this!

"So, are either of those two guys your boyfriend?" he asks, his eyes locked onto hers. Maybe he didn't notice her momentary lapse of composure. "Or the guy you were sitting with outside?"

"As a matter of fact, they all are," she replies.

Logan's hands come up to press against his chest over his heart, feigning injury. "Ouch!"

She giggles, the sound feeling more awkward and less controlled. What the hell is happening to her? "Actually, I'm single. For the moment."

They share a look, and for a few long seconds, it feels like they're alone in the frozen yogurt shop. All she can see is Logan, her eyes outlining the perfectly styled brown hair, the chiseled edges of his jaw, the bulges of his shoulders, the way his jeans hug him in all the right places. He looks like a piece of chocolate, something she hasn't let herself have for months since track season began. Even his smell is sweet and rich and tempting.

"In that case, may I join you and your friends outside?"

"Of course," she purrs, her voice coming out louder than she expected. She links her arm around his and tugs him toward the door.

Suki and Zayn are all but yelling at each other at their table, and Cassandra rolls her eyes in embarrassment. She loudly clears her throat to get their attention, then says, "Hey guys, this is Logan. Logan, this is Suki and Zayn."

He nods at both of them as he and Cassandra sit.

"Okay, bro, back me up," Zayn says, turning to Logan like they didn't just meet. "The black Super Suit is the coolest, right?"

Logan glances at Cassandra with mild amusement, then regards Zayn. "I mean, if we're talking aesthetics, I gotta go with the gold."

Both Zayn and Suki throw their hands up with exasperated scoffs, but Cassandra bites back a satisfied grin as she pokes her spoon at her non-fat froyo.

"But, to be honest," Logan continues, "I think the Super Suits in general are concerning. Sure, they may have saved us this time. But what if the people behind the masks decide to use that power against us?"

Cassandra's brows hike up skeptically. "You think the Super Suits might be dangerous?"

Logan shrugs, stirring his fruit and M&Ms into his yogurt. "I think, if they had nothing to hide, they would have come forward a long time ago. Why all the secrecy if they're not planning on using those suits for nefarious purposes in the future? They could be heroes right now."

"Um, hello, they already are," Suki says matter-of-factly. "Hiding their identities is exactly what superheroes do."

"Yeah," Zayn adds. "You think Bruce Wayne was like, 'Yo, everybody, I'm Batman'? Clark Kent, Peter Parker, Oliver Queen, Hal Jordan"—he taps a new finger with each name added to the list—"they all hid their identities so they could lead a normal life and not put their loved ones at risk."

"Good point, babe—" Suki gasps, and her eyes widen as

her face reddens. "Uh, I gotta go…" is all she says before jumping out of her chair and scurrying down the sidewalk.

"Suks, wait!" Zayn shoots up, nearly toppling his chair as he does, and runs after her.

"What was up with that?" Logan asks, looking after them.

"Don't ask." Cassandra sighs. She crosses her arms on the table and leans forward. "So, you say you've seen me here before, but I would have certainly noticed if you'd ever been in here."

"I've never actually come in," he admits. "I've only ever driven by. But today I figured, might as well try something new."

"And meet the blonde you've apparently been spying on?" she teases.

"The *hot* blonde I've apparently been spying on." He smirks.

Her heart flutters, and again, she feels strangely off balance. No guy has ever made her feel like this before. Like she's not completely in control of herself.

In an attempt to feign nonchalance, she looks down at her froyo. "You don't go to Mirror Point High. It's a small school and there's no way I've missed you. Where do you go to school?"

"I actually study at NYU," he replies.

"You live in the city?" she asks, surprised. "What brings you out here?"

He frowns, which is still somehow super handsome. "My little sister is dating a guy in the area, so I frequently have to play babysitter."

Aw, how sweet.

"I'm guessing you don't like the guy?" she hedges curiously.

"I'm the big brother. It's kinda my job not to like him." He chuckles.

This guy just keeps getting better and better. She wants to know more about him. Even though he makes her feel uncomfortable in her own skin, she can't get enough of his presence.

She asks him about college and what he's studying, and he tells her all about how boring law is but how worthwhile it will be when he can make a difference in the world. They talk for hours, about everything and about nothing. The conversation just flows so easily.

She doesn't even bother to look at the time until the sky glows orange with the setting sun.

"Oh wow, it's already five," she says, checking her phone. And she still has math homework and a paper to write. "I gotta get home."

"Can I see you again?" he asks as she slings her bag over her shoulder.

Why is she blushing? Normally, she would've written her number on the inside of his forearm before he even had a chance to ask.

"Of course," she stammers.

He hands her his phone, which is already open to the dial screen. She accepts it and types in her number, then gives it back.

"Call me," she says, wiggling her fingers goodbye before she heads to her car.

She can't help but pay attention to her feet as she walks away, which feel a bit jell-o-y. Before she gets to the driver door, her right foot catches behind her left and she stumbles forward, catching herself on the silver metal.

Getting back to her feet, she glances over her shoulder at the table. Sure enough, Logan is watching her.

Dammit, what is happening here?

Feeling like she's going to die of embarrassment, and sure that he's never going to call her now, she reluctantly opens the door and plops onto the leather seat, starting the car.

Her phone's screen illuminates in the cupholder beside her. A new text message. Trying to appear unphased and overly important in case Logan is still watching, she picks it and checks.

Dinner and a movie tomorrow? —Logan.

She slowly looks up, and Logan is smiling at her with a hopeful yet questioning expression.

Yes, she types and sends.

She watches as he looks down at his phone, and the biggest smile yet spreads across his gorgeous face. He types something, and a second later her phone lights up again.

Can't wait.

Smiling so wide that it hurts her cheeks, Cassandra pulls out and drives away.

Tomorrow can't come soon enough!

15

TRISTAN

When Tristan said he could fit through the porthole window of the attic, he was obviously being optimistic. He wriggles his shoulders, ignoring the way the curved metal of the window frame is cutting into his upper arms.

He needs to get out. Breathe some fresh air. Check on things. And the middle of the night, while the Pierce household is silent, is his best time to do that.

Feeling a little like he's being extruded, Tristan wriggles again and his torso scrapes through. He allows himself a breath, acknowledging that his widest part is through. Placing his hands on the outside wall of the house, he wonders what he's supposed to do now. Plunge headfirst to the ground below?

He grins to himself. Challenge accepted.

A bit more swaying side to side, and his hips are resting on the window sill, his arms holding him upright like he's in some half-floating yoga pose. His pulse quickens with excitement as he coils his muscles in preparation.

Here's hoping he can pull this off…

He contracts his arms like he's doing a push up and then shoves off the wall and into the night air. His legs clear the window and he tucks them in. And then he's falling, tumbling, knowing there's less than a second before he hits the ground.

Still mid-tumble, he grips his stone.

"Akash."

Before he can blink, his suit is his second skin. He powers up, soaring for the sky.

Tristan whoops, adrenaline surging through his body. He did it! Not only is he out, flying, he did it with style. Executing a quick triple barrel in celebration, he levels out and angles for home.

Conscious he's grinning like the Cheshire cat, he doesn't care. This is a great way to end an unforgettable day. Because as much fun as this was, it still doesn't compare to the day he spent with Brielle.

He's never experienced anything so...normal. His entire life has been defined by being, well, un-normal. He's always known he's not only an alien, he's a prince. One tasked with protecting the Universe. From the moment he could walk and talk, he's prepared for that. Trained for it. Forfeited the average life most other teens have.

He's never begrudged it, knowing it's a responsibility he was born into. A privilege.

But today, just sitting around and watching movies with Brielle, cooking, joking...well, that had been the most average thing he's ever done. For a few hours, there was no evil breathing down their necks. No lives to save. Just the two of them...no need to hide how they feel.

It was downright beautiful.

The thought of having more moments like that has Tristan soaring higher into the atmosphere without even realizing it. With a rueful shake of his head, he sinks back through the nighttime clouds, seeing his house up ahead.

Maybe he and Brielle could go for a fly sometime. Just the two of them. He could teach her a few tricks. He can already imagine her clinging to him, her breathless squeals tripping over his heart as he propels them through an endless barrel roll.

Although not normal by Earth standards, who knows? Maybe teens their age on their home planets do that sort of thing all the time.

Still grinning, Tristan lands on the roof of the place he finally started calling home. Quickly retracting his suit, he makes his way to the door, presses his thumb to the sensor pad and enters.

Inside, the place is quiet, but Tristan still stands at the top of the stairs, listening. He came here to make sure no one's made their way inside, whether it's FBI or Skins. But the fortress Alden built them is silent, as if it's holding its breath.

Aren't we all? Tristan thinks to himself as he jogs down the stairs.

He makes his way through the dark house, noting that nothing seems out of place. He even checks the above-stairs rooms just to make sure, but everything is just as he and Jareth left it—either uninhabited or kinda messy.

In the living room, he stops in front of the book case, taking in the photo of Zarius and Tess. Tristan can feel the same happiness bubbling through his veins that's shining from their faces.

He brushes a finger over the image. "I can see why you spent so much time in the kitchen, Zarius."

The moment the words are out, Tristan's hand drops. Zarius was the one who taught him everything he knows about the Zodiac Guardians. Including the fact there's a second Gemini out there. Waiting to be found.

One who's destined to be his soulmate.

Tristan shoves the thought away, pressing the button that will open the secret door and quickly striding down the stairs. He'll deal with that when he gets to it. Right now, it feels good that his heart and mind aren't constantly at war for once

Down in HQ, the lights come on the moment Tristan enters. He patrols the entire floor that's been built beneath the house just for good measure, but it's like walking through a tomb. The place is untouched, and a ball of tension unwinds in his chest.

It seems the FBI or the Skins haven't realized that HQ exists.

A quick check of his computer shows the scans that run twenty-four-seven haven't detected anything new. A review of the security camera history shows everything's been quiet around the place.

Tristan leans back in his chair, not sure how much of that is good news and how much is bad news. Quiet in the world of the Zodiac Guardians could be either...or both.

Spinning idly from side to side, he wonders what he should do now. He needs to get back to the attic soon, but another few minutes of dust-free air would be nice.

Tristan pulls out his cell, opening the group chat for the Zodiacs. Everyone should've received the new phones he sent them—finding the drawer full of burner phones had been another gift Alden had left behind. A quick check in on how everyone is doing, then Tristan will get going.

Y'all doing okay?

It's then that Tristan realizes the time—a little after midnight. He doubts anyone will be awake to respond.

Cassandra's reply is almost instant, though.

All quiet here. Out to the movies tomorrow. I mean, tonight.

Tristan frowns a little. *Be careful.*

I'm being a normal teen, like I'm supposed to. People our age aren't 'careful.'

Tristan rolls his eyes, figuring Cassandra just did the same. *Just watch your back.*

Because he can't be there to do it for her. Cassandra's still adjusting to life as a Zodiac. She's also the one who they need to make sure has control of her powers...

Jareth's response is next, telling Tristan that neither of his friends were asleep, despite the late hour.

All quiet here, too. But then again, I'm hanging out with a bunch of nuns...

Tristan wonders how Jareth is finding Grace Orphanage. It's the place he might've grown up in if he wasn't adopted. In fact, it's where Brielle grew up. He quickly types a response.

Do you need anything?

If you see any wanted posters with my face on them, take them down.

Tristan frowns. The fact that the FBI tried to nab Jareth shows that Jack is no longer upholding the fragile truce they'd agreed on. That would be a difficult space for Veronica to navigate. What's more, the moment Jareth resisted arrest, he became more than just a person of interest. Somehow, Tristan will have to take care of Jack. It's just figuring out how...

Will do, he types. *Just make like a lobster and lay low. We'll figure something out.*

What about you? Jareth responds. *Any news?*

Cassandra jumps in before Tristan can reply. *Yeah? How's Brielle's attic?*

The innuendo is unmistakable. What makes it worse is that it's justified. He waits a few moments, but Brielle hasn't joined the chat. She's the smart one in their group and is actually asleep. Tristan sighs, deciding he wants to be open and transparent.

Brielle and I have decided to give things a go.

About freaking time!!! Cassandra responds.

Tristan waits to see what Jareth will say.

Good. Now you'll actually smile for a change. There's a pause. *Veronica's here. She said the exact same as Cass.*

Nothing serious. Tristan clarifies. *We're just going to keep it casual.*

Veronica's face appears at the top of the chat. *Sure you are...*

His cheeks a little pink, Tristan decides it's time to finish this little convo. *Anyway, I'm glad everyone's doing okay. Stay alert and stay safe.*

Jareth quickly replies. *Sure thing. Look after yourself, bro.*

Tell Sister Agatha I said hi! Cassandra adds. *I'm off to bed, I'm not going to the movies with bags under my eyes!*

Tristan's about to tuck his phone back in his pocket when one more message comes through. It seems Veronica wants to have the last word.

Tristan's going to be fine. He's going to be too busy keeping it 'casual.'

Deciding he's not going to respond to that, Tristan leaves HQ. Although things are far from perfect, they could be worse. Trekking back up the stairs to the roof, he decides he'll take quiet as a good sign. Quiet means the Zodiacs are safe. And quiet means he might have another day like the one he did with Brielle...

His cell buzzes and he wonders whether Veronica couldn't help but have another jibe. But when he looks down, there's no name waiting to be read. No familiar face smiling at him. Frowning, Tristan's flicks his thumb over the screen. Only the Zodiacs know this number.

Getting an anonymous text is never a good thing in his world.

The black typed words on the glowing background have him stopping. Stilling.

The frown deepening into a scowl.

The wormhole is growing and releasing more radiation. Do something.

.

16

LOGAN

Logan already knows a lot about Cassandra. Her father is a business mogul who seems to have done quite well from the near-catastrophe of the asteroid. Her mother is a socialite who has a penchant for travel. Cassandra goes to Mirror Point High where she cleans up each year at the awards ceremony. She represents the school in track. She has several friends who party a whole lot more than she does.

And she hasn't been around Tristan Ayers or his associates for a few days now.

But after sitting in a movie theater with her for two hours, he's learned so much more. He knows she empathized with the heroine of the thriller they watched, because although she presented as calm, Cassandra felt everything the woman did. She never jumped once, didn't squeal or close her eyes or flinch, but Logan felt her every internal startle, gasp, or held breath as a murderer was on the loose.

As much as he doesn't like to admit it, it has him respecting her. She's not simpering or coy. Cassandra is someone who holds her own.

As he waits in the foyer for her to finish in the bathroom

before they head for dinner, Logan admits he's learned a few other things. He knows she's flirty and sexy and confident. He's felt her attraction to him.

And he's definitely noticed his attraction to her.

Keeping his face neutral even though he's frowning inside, he admits that's a complication he could do without. One he won't be mentioning to his father. And one that he won't be letting get in the way of what he needs to find out.

How Cassandra fits in with this alien Zodiac threat.

But as she walks around the corner, all thoughts of... anything evaporate. In the same way he was struck dumb when she met him outside the movie theatre, Logan blinks. Then blinks again.

Her floral, red dress hugs her figure in all the right places, yet the soft skirt floats around her slim legs in ways that keep drawing his eyes there. That's when he can tear his gaze away from her face, though. Those sapphire eyes of hers are like a sparkling, seductive pool he has to stop himself from plunging into head first.

She stops in front of him. "All done. Shall we get going?"

Without realizing what he's doing until he's done it, Logan draws in a breath, inhaling her sweet, slightly spiced scent. "There's a nice little place not far from here. We can walk?"

Those blue eyes of hers sparkle. "Great idea."

They leave the movie theatre, finding twilight has descended outside as they fall into step on the sidewalk.

"What did you think of the movie?" he asks.

Cassandra angles her head, her thick waves of blonde hair slipping over her shoulder—the one that's bare apart from the thin strap of her dress. "I liked it. Interesting choice for a first date movie," she teases. "Trying to scare me off?"

He was trying to see what her reaction would be. Scared

and simpering as she clung to his arm? Or would she hate it but say she loved it?

Turns out, it was neither.

Logan grins. "I hope not."

She wrinkles her nose, the space between the two of them shrinking. "I'm tougher than that."

Focusing ahead, Logan acknowledges he's realizing that.

A woman walks past and he instinctively shifts closer to Cassandra so the stranger has more room. His hand brushes hers, their fingers tangling. The touch is so electrifying that Logan finds he doesn't want to let go. It seems Cassandra doesn't either, because her hand draws his in and they clasp. Logan keeps his gaze straight ahead as he swallows. A warm flurry of tingles he's never felt before are dancing up his arm and spiraling through his chest.

But holding hands is outside his brief. It implies emotional connection. A commitment he can't give. One that he's only going to betray.

Except, the more comfortable they are with each other, the more Cassandra is likely to talk. The more likely he is to get answers.

His heart thumping with too much emotion, Logan's fingers tighten around hers. Their palms connect, the tingles now so strong he can't tell whether they're coming from him or Cassandra.

They reach the door of the restaurant and Logan releases the contact, relieved but also aware that his hand suddenly feels empty. Inside, a waiter takes them to a booth.

He holds out a menu for Cassandra. "I'd be happy to tell you about our specials," he practically purrs.

Logan stills the moment his butt hits the seat. Seriously? The waiter is busting a move on a girl who's clearly on a date?

"The ones on the board?" Logan asks sharply. "We can read, thanks."

The waiter barely glances at Logan. "Well, the pasta carbonara is pretty freaking awesome."

With a wink, the guy's gone, but Logan still hasn't moved. He felt a flash of something from Cassandra when the waiter spoke. A small jolt of delight that was quickly quashed, but one nonetheless.

She likes him flirting with her?

Telling himself he's glad—finding reasons not to like Cassandra is exactly what he needs right now—Logan focuses on the menu. "What do you think you'll get?"

Cassandra's brows pucker as she chews on her lip. "The Caesar salad. But easy on the dressing."

He arches a brow. "You don't want the carbonara?"

The moment he says the words, he wishes he could take them back. He sounds like a jealous boyfriend!

But Cassandra shakes her head. "Too many carbs. No real nutrition," she says as if by rote. She shrugs like it doesn't matter. "Besides, isn't it a rule that you don't have pasta on a first date? Too messy."

Although her face doesn't change, regret floats through her, only to be quickly dampened. It hits Logan that it wasn't the waiter that had something in Cassandra leaping. It was the carb loaded meal! And she's either not ordering it because she doesn't want to give the waiter any wrong signals, or she's watching what she eats.

The waiter returns and Logan shoves the menus at him, forcing the guy to look at him. "We'll have two of the carbonara, thanks. And two Cokes." Cassandra opens her mouth but Logan quickly continues. "One diet."

The waiter bristles, turning to Cassandra. "Is that okay with you?"

Cassandra leans her chin on her hand as she smiles up at

him. "It's like he can read my mind," she says, her gaze flickering to Logan. "He knew exactly what I wanted."

The waiter flushes bright red and leaves. Logan finds himself grinning as Cassandra turns back to him. She knew the waiter was flirting with her but she communicated very clearly she's here with him.

Crossing her arms on the table, she leans forward. "You're very perceptive," she observes.

Logan has to hold his smile in place otherwise it would fall away. She's right. He's always been good at reading people and sensing how they're feeling. His father has commented that it will be a strength of his as an agent. But he's surprised she noticed.

She cocks her head teasingly. "You don't have a superpower, do you? One where you can read minds?"

Logan laughs. "No superpowers here. You've been watching the Super Suits too much."

She rolls her eyes. "I'm so over that story. No one's seen them since, surely it's got to be old news soon."

Logan keeps his posture casual even though he's on high alert. "You haven't joined a fan club?"

"Nope," Cassandra says as she holds his gaze. "We'll probably never see them again."

Logan's about to ask her more about that when the waiter appears with their drinks. Cassandra barely glances at him, and Logan can't help the small spurt of warmth that sparks within him.

She flicks her thick hair over her shoulder. "So, tell me about your family. Are you and your sister close?"

"Yeah," he says casually. "We are." Or, they used to be... Until Veronica ran off and betrayed them. "It's just us two and our dad. Mom died when we were young."

Cassandra's pretty face crinkles with compassion. "I'm sorry to hear that."

"What about you? Are you close with your parents?"

Her gaze slips away. "Only when we're in the same room." She waves a dismissive hand. "I'm adopted, so I don't need to worry about anything being hereditary, though."

Despite the joke and the show that it doesn't matter, Logan senses the hurt. And the hard core of anger beneath it. Without realizing he's doing it, he leans forward and clasps her hand. "Family can be complicated."

Her gaze connects with his and stays there. The warmth their touch seems to spark curls around them, feeling like it's drawing him in closer. Logan knows he should pull away. That he's getting in too deep.

But he can't.

What's worse, he doesn't want to.

The waiter arrives again, holding two large plates. "Two carbonaras," he says sullenly as he slips them on the table between Logan and Cassandra.

They draw back, their gazes falling away. Logan notes Cassandra's cheeks are a little pink, as if she's been thrown by how intense the moment was, too. Each time it's so powerful, he can't tell where his feelings begin and hers end.

"I can't remember the last time I had pasta," she murmurs. Digging in her fork, she twirls it around in the fettuccini.

Logan's about to load his own up when he sees that she's raising the ball of pasta to her mouth. Riveted, he stops to watch.

Cassandra's eyes close as her lush lips open, bliss already lighting her features. Her mouth closes around the fettuccini and she withdraws the fork.

Sweet Lord, since when did pasta become so sensual?

Her eyes shoot open as a length of creamy noodle slips out. She quickly sucks it in and it whips her chin on the way up. Cassandra's eyes widen with embarrassment, her cheeks flushing a delectable red as she places her hand over her mouth. "I told you it was too messy!" she squeaks.

Logan laughs, but it's a laugh that he hasn't experienced in a very long time. It's a genuine one, full of humor and delight and the desire to feel like this forever. Cassandra bursts into her own peals of giggles as she scrambles for a napkin.

Logan picks up his own and reaches over, wiping away the smear of creamy sauce. The sounds of their joy fade away as their electric attraction, one that seems to need very little touch to fuel it, flares again.

"This way, please," the waiter says loudly.

He seats a father and a girl about twelve years old, at the table beside them.

Logan draws back, starting to think the dude's doing it on purpose. He clears his throat, focusing back on his food. He should be grateful. He needs to get his head back in the game. His father recruited him to Nebula, for Pete's sake.

"So, are Suki and Zayn an item again?"

"Wow, you remembered," Cassandra says, clearly impressed.

Logan shrugs. "I have a good memory for detail."

For those who are his mark, he reminds himself.

"Yep, they're conjoined twins again, locked at the lips." She wrinkles her nose as she smiles. "It's pretty gross. I tend to not be where they are."

"So, who do you hang out with at school then?" Logan asks, winding more pasta on his fork like he's not paying close attention to this answer. Cassandra and Tristan are friends. He wouldn't be here if they weren't. Ignoring the pang that thought causes, Logan watches Cassandra with casual interest.

"Whoever's around," she replies breezily. "I'm busy a lot of the time with study or track, so I don't mind."

Not the answer he was looking for. Logan's loading up his fork again as he wonders what his next angle could be, but it suddenly strikes him that maybe there's nothing to find.

Maybe Cassandra has nothing to do with any of this.

The clamp around his chest loosens, falling away like an unwanted shackle. Maybe there's absolutely no reason he can't continue to see her…

Realizing their meal is almost over, and that he doesn't want this evening to end yet, Logan keeps his gaze on his food as he asks the next question. "So, did you want to go for a walk after this? Maybe grab some dessert over at Creamy Dreams?"

There's silence and an unwilling flush climbs up his neck. Now that he's not playing the part of information seeker, this just got harder. Rejection is going to sting a whole lot more.

He looks up when she doesn't answer, ready to retract the offer. He's pushed too soon. Gone in too hard.

But Cassandra's not paying attention; in fact, he doubts she heard him. What's more, her hands are gripping the table as her unfocused gaze stares to the left. Logan glances that way, noting the father is talking to his daughter at the table behind them.

"Do I get dessert?" the little girl asks excitedly.

"You know the answer to that, Charlotte. Not when you got a B on your latest test."

Logan hides his surprise. This girl would still be in elementary school.

Her face falls. "But I studied real hard. I promise I did."

The man flicks his napkin sharply before slipping it on his lap. "Well, next time you'll study harder."

Asshole, Logan thinks with a flash of disgust.

"But—"

"We'll talk about this at home," the man says in a low voice.

Cassandra's sharp indrawn breath is followed by a piercing bolt of fear. And then the anger's back, hot and fluid and swift.

The man stands, the napkin flopping back onto the table. "I'm going to the bathroom, and when I come back, I want you to tell me which piece you've chosen for your piano recital."

The man stalks past and Cassandra visibly tightens.

Logan frowns. "Is everything okay?"

Cassandra's spine straightens as she snaps to attention. She slams her hands into her lap. "Oh, sorry! I was just thinking about an...assignment that I'd forgotten about!" She smiles brightly. "One I really need to get working on."

"Like, now?"

"Yep!" Cassandra shoots to her feet. "I'm so sorry. I really was having a great time."

"Ah, sure." Logan stands, too, leaving some bills on the table to pay for dinner. Confused, he tries to figure out what's going on. Why would overhearing an asshat dad have her so flustered? Or did she hear the invite for the walk...

"Just give me a sec," Cassandra says, that megawatt fluorescent smile still in place.

She turns away, flicking open her purse, and Logan wonders if she's about to pay for her half of the meal. Knowing he might be being old-fashioned, but not caring, his objection is cut off as Cassandra hurries to the girl. She leans down, passing her a ten dollar note.

"B's deserve dessert," she whispers. "Get yourself something yummy another time."

The little girl beams, her eyes wide as she quickly disappears the bill into her pocket.

Barely glancing at Logan, and not waiting for the thank

you the little girl is about to blurt, Cassandra heads for the door. "Let's get going."

Logan stays where he is, pleased shock rooting him to the spot. That's why she wanted to leave? So she could do something nice for the little girl?

Has he ever seen a girl do something so sexy?

He's about to turn away, a flush of something new and warm filling his chest, when he stops.

He stills. His brows slam down. The warmth cools.

Cassandra's side of the table has been altered.

Two sets of finger marks have been singed into the table-top, in the same place she was gripping it. Logan blinks, trying to wash the sight away, but the charred lines are still there.

If he were anyone else, he could explain it away. They were already there. There's no way someone could do that.

But he's not. He's Jack Cadbury's son. He's an agent of Nebula. He knows aliens exist.

Cold, hard truth settles in Logan's gut as bile stings the back of his throat.

There's no way Cassandra can be human.

BRIELLE

B rielle is floating on air all day Sunday as she helps
Frank fill out paperwork. Yesterday with Tristan had
been heavenly, and the warmth of that bliss still resonates
inside her chest as if Tristan were still holding her, his lips
just a breath away.

As she fills in the name Joshua Stein for the umpteenth
time on this fund redistribution form, she wonders how
Tristan is doing up in the attic. Is he comfortable? Does he
miss her? Is he thinking about her as much as she's thinking
about him?

"How ya doin' over there?" Frank asks, bending his
fingers backward to stretch them.

"Great," she says cheerily.

A faint twinge of surprise flares his eyebrows. "You're
better with paperwork than I am." He closes one of his hands
and pushes the other palm against the knuckles, releases a
series of cracks like the sound of popcorn popping in the
microwave. "Looks like I hired the right girl." He winks.

"Thanks." She beams. "I'm just happy I can help. And I
really don't mind paperwork so much. It's so mindless, I

actually find it relaxing. Like washing dishes or folding laundry."

He gives her a look like she's a unicorn that just walked into their backyard. "I swear, I adopted the perfect child!"

She giggles and shakes her head.

"Bri?"

The sound of Bea's voice has both of them looking up toward the door of Frank's office. Brielle doesn't recognize the concerned note until she sees her mom in the doorway, with two men in black suits standing behind her on either side, their hands clasped in front of them, eyes fixed on her.

Brielle's heart stops, her lungs forgetting how to function. Her cheeks go cold as she's sure every ounce of blood has drained from her face.

Tristan! She pleads inwardly, a prayer that he will somehow escape the attic before they find him.

Frank stands, his hands flat on the desk as he leans forward. "Can we help you gentlemen?" His voice holds the same note of caution as Bea's.

"We have reason to believe that your daughter, Brielle, might have some information about a suspected terrorist," says the man to Bea's right.

Frank and Bea exchange a wide-eyed glance before turning to Brielle, who is struggling between relief that they're not here for Tristan and fresh terror that they've come for her instead. Frank takes a step sideways along the desk, putting himself in front of Brielle.

"Is she in any trouble?" he asks.

"Not yet," says the first agent.

"We just need her to come in and answer a few questions," the other says before the first finishes. "As long as she answers truthfully, she'll be free to go."

"And who decides if she's being truthful?" Bea asks, stepping to the side and pinning the men with untrusting eyes.

"Bea," Frank cautions, shaking his head warningly. But Brielle is impressed by Bea's brazenness. This is a side of her mom she hasn't seen before, and it makes Brielle love and respect her so much more. Frank regards the agents again. "As her legal guardians, I'm sure we're allowed to come with her."

The men look at each other, then the left one shrugs. "That would be fine."

"Your daughter will ride with us and you can follow in your car," adds the other.

Arms crossed, Bea closes in on them. "No. One of us is going to be in the car with her."

The men share another look, then without a word both nod in agreement.

"Miss Pierce," the man on the right beckons, and Brielle obediently rises from the desk and follows them out of the house.

There's a black SUV parked in the driveway, just like the one she saved Tristan from. She wonders if these are the same federal agents who tried to arrest him, wonders if they recognize her from before they got their butts kicked. But she never got a good look at their faces in the dark, and she hopes that if these are the same agents, the same was true for them.

They open the back door and Brielle ducks inside without a word. Bea follows, but stops halfway through the door to look at Frank.

"I'll be right behind you," he calls before running to the garage to get the car.

Bea sits down and the agent closes the door loudly. The vehicle pulls out of the driveway, and Bea's hand finds Brielle's and covers it, squeezing it reassuringly. She doesn't ask any questions, doesn't say anything, but Brielle can tell that the words are swirling behind her closed lips, aching to come out but afraid of incriminating Brielle further.

The drive is silent, and the late afternoon sun stains Brielle's vision with green dots as she stares out the window, trying to figure out how she's going to get out of this.

She can't lie. She's pretty sure by now that ability has been trained out of her. And she can't simply not answer their questions. Is she skilled enough at giving half-truths to get away with keeping the secrets of the Zodiacs? If they ask her a direct question, she'll be forced to give a direct answer. Omission won't work.

Bea's grasp on her hands tightens the closer they get to New York City. Her presence is an unbelievable comfort, but at the same time, it makes Brielle's stomach twist into bigger knots. If she's forced into spilling her secrets, her parents will be there to hear all of it. They'll find out just how much she's been keeping from them. They'll never forgive her.

She should have insisted they stay home, but she'd been too stunned and muted by fear to do or say anything.

Brielle has always felt an instinctual guilt whenever she's accused of doing something she didn't do, as if just the accusation itself makes her the perpetrator. But that's nothing compared to the true guilt of being accused of something she absolutely did do. For the first time in her life, she's legitimately in trouble for something she did that seems wrong to those in charge, and the turmoil writhing inside her gut is almost unbearable.

By the time they get to the FBI building, the roads are lit by artificial orange lights, the sun long disappeared over the towering skyscrapers and tall apartments that litter the city. They are in the heart of New York City, far from the dilapidated and dreary neighborhood of the Gym, and it feels strange to be in the artificial day created by the streetlamps reflecting all the way up the mile-stretching glass windows that keep the night sky so far away.

The agents open the door on Brielle's side and escort her and Bea toward the entrance. Frank catches up not long after and they all go inside. Despite the early evening hour, a time when most business should be closing, the large lobby is bustling with activity. Smartly dressed men and women come and go, speaking very business-like into cell phones, holstering guns on their hips as they exit, or towing hand-cuffed criminals into secured rooms much like the one to which she suspects she's about to be led.

"This way," says one of the agents, marshalling her across the giant blue and yellow FBI logo on the shining linoleum floor.

She swallows as they enter a narrow hallway lined with doors, trying desperately to remind herself that she's not a criminal. She's done nothing wrong. All she's ever done was fight to protect the Universe against those who would destroy it. She's not the bad guy.

But the fact that she wasn't brought here in handcuffs like the other people in these rooms does little to assuage her ridiculous guilt and fear.

They stop in front of a door at the end of the long hall, and one of the agents slides a plastic card down the scanner that stands guard where the doorknob should be. A little green light flashes, the lock *clicks*, and the door pops open just a crack. The agent pulls it open and gestures for Brielle to precede him into the room, which is barren save for the single steel table bolted to the floor and a plastic chair on either side of it.

Bea and Frank attempt to follow her in, but the second agent stops them. "We can't allow either of you to interfere with the interrogation. You can watch from the other room."

He points to the mirror on the wall, which obviously doubles as a window.

Bea's face hardens and her eyes narrow at the man. Then she shoots Brielle a glance that is full of love and support, and says, "We'll be just on the other side."

Brielle nods, and the door closes, leaving her alone in this sterile, cold room.

She moves to the table and sits in the chair opposite the mirror, tucking her shaky hands between her wobbly thighs for warmth.

Just breathe. Everything will be alright. Everything will be alright... she repeats in her head, trying to calm herself with a mantra she doesn't believe.

After only a few seconds of waiting—though it feels like forever—the door opens, and even though she knew who it was going to be, who it had to be, the sight of his unshaven face makes her heart somersault.

Detective Jack Cadbury takes the seat across from her and folds his arms over the top of the table. His expression is unreadable, and Brielle tries to copy his example. She refuses to let him see how shaken she is to be here under his penetrating espresso gaze.

"Hello, Miss Pierce," he begins, his voice far from cheerful. "I'd say it's a pleasure to see you again, but I'm sure neither of us agrees with that statement."

Brielle keeps her gaze steady on him. "How can I help you, Detective?"

"Your known associate, Tristan Ayers, is suspected of being involved in terrorist activity," he begins, sitting back in his chair. "When we attempted to bring him in for questioning, he assaulted two of our agents and ran. Since then, he has not returned to his residence and has been absent from school."

He pauses, watching Brielle like a vulture waiting for a wounded gazelle to die.

Brielle feigns shock half a second too late. "Wow. I... I had noticed he wasn't at school, but..." she moistens her lips, but her entire mouth is dry, too. Mostly, she's stalling, trying to find things to say that are non-incriminating while still true. "Maybe he misunderstood the situation, thought your agents were trying to hurt him." There was certainly the possibility at the time that they could have been Skins trying to capture or kill him.

Jack narrows his eyes and shakes his head ever so slightly. "No, he understood the situation perfectly, and he still incapacitated two of our best operatives." He leans forward and continues before she can say anything else in Tristan's defense. "I didn't bring you in to debate the innocence of Tristan Ayers. You're here because you are his closest known associate, and we have reason to believe you may know where he's hiding."

He laces his fingers in front of him and flares his bushy brows at her expectantly.

It wasn't actually a question but a statement. So she has some wiggle room with how she can respond.

"What about Jareth Stone?" she asks, keeping her voice as smooth as she can manage. "The two of them live together. If anyone knows where Tristan is, I'm sure Jareth does."

Jack frowns, his coffee eyes swirling with disbelief at her ignorance of Jareth's situation. "Jareth Stone, who is equally suspected, also escaped arrest and hasn't been seen since. I'm sure you've noticed him missing from school as well."

Brielle shrugs, hoping it comes off as genuine confusion. "He doesn't have the best attendance, so him missing a day or two isn't all that noticeable."

She takes in a long breath, priding herself for doing this

well so far. Evasion is a skill she's honed all her life to avoid having to lie.

Jack lets out a gravely sigh, the frustration clear in the way the vein protrudes over his temple. "Have either Tristan Ayers or Jareth Stone tried to contact you in the last forty-eight hours?"

And there it is. A direct question.

"No, they have not," she replies, her voice clear and even.

Technically, it's true. Tristan has not tried to contact her —any interaction they've had has been initiated by her. And it wasn't Jareth who reached out to let them know about his whereabouts, it was Veronica.

"What exactly are they suspected of, anyway? They're a couple of teenage boys." She's baiting him, trying to get him to admit his perceived insane alien theories in front of the agents and her parents that are listening on the other side of the one-way mirror. It might discredit this entire investigation if his superiors overhear.

"We've had our eyes on Tristan Ayers for several years," he explains. "He's been linked to many incidents during that time, including the murder of his parents a few months ago."

"Tristan did *not* kill his parents." Her retort is immediate and passionate.

"That's still to be determined," he says calmly.

"And anyway, he didn't even know Jareth when his parents were killed," she argues. "So, why are you after both of them?"

He lifts one of his thick eyebrows. "I think you know why." He leans closer and says in a lower register, "You're just lucky we don't have the evidence to implicate you, too."

White hot panic bolts up her spine. They have evidence on Tristan and Jareth.

"Evidence of what?" she asks.

"Okay. Fine. I'll play along." He leans back again and

crosses his arms, puffing out his chest like a rooster. "We have evidence that the two of them were involved with the Super Suits and the asteroid explosion."

A nervous laugh escapes, and she plays it off as dubious. "You really think two orphaned teenage boys have the resources to build hi-tech weapons like the Super Suits? That's the wildest rumor I've heard yet."

"You and I both know they're not just any average teenage boys," he says. "And I suspect you're not just an average teenage girl, either."

"Then what are we?" she dares.

Say it. Say the word...

But something else happens, something all too familiar, and as usual with the worst possible timing.

The edges of her vision blur as the vibration rattles her skull. And suddenly, she's no longer in the chair in the cramped windowless room. In fact, she's not even her.

She's someone else, driving down a long stretch of road. The hands that hold onto the steering wheel are large with hairy knuckles.

Out of nowhere, something streaks across the road and crashes into the grass with a blaze and loud *boom*, causing the large hands in front of her to grip at the wheel and veer it violently to the right to avoid collision. The eyes she's seeing through rush out of the car and run toward the crash site.

To Brielle's astonishment, the object buried half way into the cratered ground is a pearly white space pod, just like the one Tristan showed her.

She's moving closer, walking all around the pod. There's a *pop*, and she's backing away as the top of the pod opens upward. A full grown man emerges, climbing his way out of the dark earth. She's standing still as if frozen, her vision fixed on this man.

Until he stands up and spots her. The hands attached to her rise up, clasping a gun and aiming it right at the man.

"Freeze!" Jack's voice orders.

Faster than lightning, the man raises a far superior gun and shoots a blast of light at her. She dodges just in time but is suddenly tackled to the ground.

All goes black for a moment.

Then the vision has her waking, propping herself up on the ground. And the pod is gone.

Brielle is suddenly back in her chair in the tiny interrogation room, and she knows two things. One: Jack saw one of the pods land here from the Gemini Space Station seventeen years ago. And Two: the man who emerged from that pod was Alden.

"Did you hear me, Miss Pierce?" Jack asks, a wild look in his eyes.

She realizes she's missed something during her vision, and she hopes she hasn't given anything away.

"Sorry?" she mutters, shaking her head.

"Do you know where Tristan Ayers and Jareth Stone are hiding?" he repeats, enunciating each word with annoyance.

Another direct question. And there's no way to half-truth her way out of this one. Her throat tightens in refusal to speak a falsehood, her guts tingling in anticipation of the guilt she doesn't want to feel. Her mind rapidly flips through possible responses until it finds the perfect distraction.

"Have you asked your daughter?" she asks coolly, and the way his eyes widen tell her she's struck a chord. "Veronica? She's dating Jareth. She might know where he's hiding?"

Jack jumps to his feet and slams his hand onto the center of the table, the sudden *bang* making her flinch and retreat against the back of the chair. "If you know anything about where my daughter is, you'd better tell me *right now!*" he barks, his index finger pointed threateningly toward her face.

"I haven't seen Veronica in days!" Brielle squeaks defensively. "I swear!"

"Tell me where Tristan and Jareth are!" Jack barks.

Just lie, she tells herself. *You can do it. It's so easy for everyone else. It can be for you, too. So you'll feel guilty. Big deal.*

She opens her mouth, but still, her throat constricts as she prepares to say she doesn't know. Three little words, and they cling to the tip of her tongue in desperation not to be voiced.

The door opens, and a tall, lanky man with salt-and-pepper hair in a gray suit enters with a briefcase in one hand.

"Who the hell are you?" Jack snaps at him, a little ragged.

"I am Solomon Gray, Miss Pierce's lawyer," the man announces with a charming southern drawl. "And, unless you are charging my client with a crime, I demand she be released at once."

Brielle stares at this stranger, stunned into silence.

Did her parents contact him? Maybe Frank did on the drive over?

"We're not done here," Jack grumbles.

"Now, my client has answered all of your questions," Solomon says. "She hasn't been contacted by Tristan Ayers or Jareth Stone since their disappearance. And she hasn't seen your daughter in several days. If this is all a matter of your daughter running away, I think you might look to yourself for the problem—"

"Watch it, pal!" Jack growls.

"Is it my client under arrest?" Solomon presses.

Jack glares at him, gritting his teeth.

"Is she?" Solomon repeats.

"No," Jack finally relents.

"Very well." He opens his arm toward Brielle. "Miss Pierce, I believe you're free to go."

Brielle gets up and gratefully rushes to the door.

Jack cuts her off, blocking her way. "If you do hear from either of the fugitives, or Veronica, I trust you'll contact me immediately. If you fail to report any such activity, you will be aiding and abetting, and I can arrest you for that."

All the while, his breath is hot on her face, saturating the air around her with the stench of stale coffee, so she holds her mouth shut and simply nods before sliding past him into the hall.

Frank and Bea are already waiting there, and she runs into their arms.

"Thank you guys for calling Solomon," Brielle gushes.

"We didn't call him," Frank says with a confused furrow in his forehead, and Bea shakes her head.

"Well, if you didn't..." She turns around, looking for the lawyer who got her out. But he's nowhere in sight.

Who did?

18

LOGAN

C assandra is laughing as she enters the school building, her smile flashing at the jock she's walking beside. Logan narrows his gaze as he chews on his lip. She presents as the average, carefree teen. With a flick of her blonde hair, she disappears through the front door, off to a day of classes, laughing, and excelling.

Except below it all, she's worried. A tense feeling is gnawing at her, which is why she probably glanced both ways before sashaying through the door.

Because she's an alien.

Logan takes a sip of his coffee, grimacing. He can't under-stand what his dad sees in the stuff, but after spending the night in his car—his new home-away-from-home—watching Cassandra's house then the wakeup juice is necessary.

Plus, sleep has been elusive since their date. Cassandra is beautiful. Intriguing and funny and sassy. The one person he's ever felt so drawn to.

And she's his enemy.

The one his father has been hunting most of his career.

The image of the finger marks singed into the table has never been far from Logan's mind. He needs to tell his father. They need to bring Cassandra in for questioning.

Slugging down the last mouthful, Logan crushes the cup in his hand, instantly regretting the action. The sounds of its destruction remind him too much of what he needs to do—destroy Cassandra's life.

Because it won't stop at the questioning. There will be an arrest. Interrogations that will only intensify if she doesn't talk. Ultimately, she'll be Jack Cadbury's first big break.

And Logan will have to watch it all. He just hopes the knowledge that he's been a part of saving the world will be enough to alleviate the jagged regret he'll be carrying for the rest of his life.

And yet, he hasn't done it. Cassandra's at school, enjoying another day of freedom.

Making Logan just as much a traitor as his sister is.

His jaw tightens as he throws the cup onto the pile of trash on the passenger side floor. He hasn't done it because Cassandra's not evil. Not like the guy Logan and his dad questioned. That guy had been full of...nothing. Maybe a thin vein of guilt, definitely some low lying anger, but the dominant, blanket emotion was...darkness. Nothingness. There wasn't the passion and fire that Logan's sensed in Cassandra. The very same things he's so drawn to.

His cell rings, snapping him out of the never ending merry-go-round of confusion that he keeps finding himself in. Seeing it's his father, he quickly answers.

"Hey, Dad."

"Brielle got away," his father states flatly.

Logan straightens in his seat. "She ran, too?"

Tristan and Jareth disappeared like the cowards they are. Logan's hand tightens around his phone. Except Jareth took Veronica with him.

"No," his father growls. "We brought her in for questioning. She wouldn't give me a straight answer. The moment it looked like I was about to get somewhere, some asshole lawyer came in and whisked her away."

"Dammit," Logan mutters.

A small part of him was hoping they'd get the answers he needed and he wouldn't be the one to betray Cassandra.

"Yeah. We're getting close, Logan, I can feel it."

Logan's eyes flutter closed. They're far closer than his father realizes. He opens his mouth, loyalty to this determined man with a heart the size of the very planet he's always fought to save winning out.

"I've got a lead, though," his father says before he gets a chance to speak. "I'm sending you a photo of the lawyer. He called himself Solomon. See if you can find out anything."

Logan's cell dings. "Can do," he says, relieved that he has something else he can focus on.

"Thanks," his father says. "Have you found anything?"

The short-lived relief promptly dies. "I'm not sure yet," he says before he can stop himself. "There hasn't been any direct link to Ayers so far."

His father grunts. "He's going to have to show himself sooner or later."

Suppressing a sigh, Logan knows what he's expected to say next. "I'll continue to keep an eye on Cassandra."

"Maybe meet with her again. I'm not convinced Miss Pretty and Popular isn't involved in this somehow."

It's ironic that his father's instincts are something Logan's always admired about him. The very same instincts that now have Logan in the predicament he's in.

"Will do," he says, knowing it's a request but it feels far more like an order. One he no longer wants to carry out.

With a quick goodbye, they hang up. Logan's head falls to the steering wheel with a thud.

He needs to see Cassandra again. The thought has his heart soaring in ways it really shouldn't.

His cell rings again and Logan automatically picks it up, assuming it's his father. But it's a familiar female voice that greets him.

"Hey, Logan," Veronica says cautiously.

Logan grips the steering wheel, hot anger flushing through him. "Where the hell are you?"

"So you can tell Dad? I don't think so," she says archly, but her words are quickly followed by a sigh. "I'm safe, okay?"

"You're with him, aren't you?" Logan almost can't bring himself to say his name. "Jareth."

"Because he's not the bad guy here!" Veronica half-shouts. "He hasn't done anything wrong."

"Apart from evading arrest."

"Because you two have jumped to an incredibly incorrect conclusion," his sister snaps back instantly.

Logan rubs his forehead in frustration. "How could you do this to him, KitKat?"

"I love Dad as much as you do," she huffs angrily, but Logan doesn't need to be near her to sense the hurt. He knows Veronica too well.

He sighs. "I know you do."

That's why none of this makes sense.

"I want to make this right," she says quietly. "I just don't know how."

The sincerity in Veronica's voice tugs at Logan's heart. None of them like what's happening to their family right now.

He rubs his forehead even harder. "I have an idea."

"You do?" The spark in his sister's voice is enough to have Logan hoping he's making the right call.

"There's a lawyer guy who's popped up. He said he's representing Brielle."

"Really?" The surprise in that one word is enough to tell Logan that his sister didn't know about this.

"Yeah. Dad sent me his photo, taken from the FBI security cameras. He wants me to find out what I can." He can't quite believe he's about to do this. "I'll send it to you. See if that clever nose of yours can sniff anything out."

There's a pause on the other side of the line and Logan holds his breath. If Solomon helped Brielle out, then it's likely he's connected to the Zodiacs somehow. If Veronica is, too, then there's no way she'll take this on.

"You'd do this for me?" she asks quietly.

Logan grits his teeth. "Of course. And for Dad." And the family they can all feel crumbling apart. "We need to stick together, KitKat."

Veronica sniffs. "I know. I want that, too." There's a shuffle, as if she's wiping her nose, and she speaks again, this time her voice far stronger. "I won't let you down. Solomon now has a great big target on his back."

Logan allows himself a smile. His sister's tenacity is only seconded by their father's. "Poor guy."

"I'll keep you posted," she says cheerily and hangs up.

Logan stares at his phone.

We need to stick together.

His father and Veronica are the only family he has. How could he have forgotten that?

His thumbs quickly fly over the screen as he types out a message.

Hey gorgeous girl, whatcha doing?

He doesn't expect a quick reply seeing as Cassandra would be in class, but his phone dings almost instantly.

Oh, so you haven't ghosted me!

Logan flushes a little. If this were any other circumstance, he would've had to stop himself from texting Cassandra three minutes after they said goodbye at the end of their date.

Sorry, things have been a bit intense lately. Let me make it up to you?

Well, I am VERY hurt...

Logan doesn't realize he's grinning until he catches his reflection in the windscreen. Quickly quashing it, he types a reply. *Challenge accepted. I'll pick you up at six?*

He presses send and waits.

It's a date.

Dammit. The grin is back.

19

TRISTAN

When Brielle first didn't answer his texts, Tristan grew impatient. He knows she has a life she needs to maintain, but…he's bored. And…he misses her.

But when she didn't respond to his calls, he became worried.

As the hours passed and evening brought its twilight shadows, he grew anxious.

Now, he's pacing the attic, wondering if he should go out and look for her. There's no way Brielle wouldn't answer for this long unless something has happened.

Cursing his confinement, Tristan spears his fingers through his hair. What if Skins have found her? What if she's hurt? Or worse…

He's just striding to the ladder—deciding there's no time to squeeze himself through the window—when he hears a car pull into the garage.

Tristan freezes, listening with every cell in his body. There's the low hum as the garage door lowers again, then a car door slamming, and another. Then one more.

Three people. Please let it be Brielle, Frank, and Bea.

But no voices seep through the walls and floors between them. Usually, there's some chatter, a laugh or two, footsteps heading straight to the kitchen. Instead, the three people entering are subdued, almost silent.

Tristan frowns, desperate to find out what's happened, but knowing he risks Brielle's parents finding out she's hidden him here if he gives into the urge and storms down there. But the not knowing is tearing him apart...

There are more footsteps and the ladder disappears as it sinks down, a square of light opening up. A moment later, Brielle is standing before him.

Without thinking, Tristan rushes forward and clasps her cheeks, needing to touch her. He studies her sweet, beautiful face. The second his gaze connects with hers, something in Tristan calms. Breathes a sigh as everything becomes right in his world.

Wordlessly, they kiss, Tristan's lips seeking the reassurance and connection he's craving. Brielle sinks against him, her hands slipping around his waist. She kisses him back as ardently as he's kissing her.

Brielle draws back an inch, face flushed as she smiles. "I missed you, too."

Tristan grins, still amazed at how good this feels. "I'm glad to see the feeling's mutual."

"It always has been," she says huskily.

Those words have Tristan's heart swelling and clenching at the same time. He pushes away any thoughts that involve the word *soulmate* before they can take hold. "Are you okay?"

She nods. "I'm fine."

"But something's happened," he states. Not only was she gone so long, Brielle's moss green eyes are tinged with uneasiness.

She sighs. "The FBI turned up. They took me in for questioning."

"They what?" Tristan draws away and starts pacing again. "Cadbury is getting too cocky. He needs to back the pitch off."

"He wanted to know where you and Jareth are. Said you're wanted in relation to terrorism charges."

Tristan snorts. "That's the best he could come up with?" He stops, turning back to Brielle. "Are you okay?"

Brielle wraps her arms around her waist. "I didn't tell him anything."

Tristan returns to stand before her. "That's not what I asked."

"It wasn't the most fun I've ever had."

Wrapping his arms around her, he draws her close, recognizing the words for what they are. An understatement. "My guess is it was hell. It's hard for you to lie."

Brielle would either have to carry the pain of the lie or live with the consequences of telling the truth—failing to protect the Zodiacs.

She presses her forehead into his chest as she clutches his shirt at his waist. "It turns out I didn't have to." She looks up, confusion adding to the unsettled currents in her eyes. "It seems I have a lawyer. A guy named Solomon turned up. He pointed out that Jack had no legal reason to hold me. The moment I was out, he disappeared."

Tristan's eyebrows shoot up. "Zarius never mentioned a lawyer."

"I didn't think so." Brielle chews her lip. "I've never seen this guy before."

"Well, that's a new development," he says thoughtfully. Who the pitch is this guy? And can they assume he's friend rather than foe? Filing that away as another question to answer, Tristan rubs his thumb over the small of Brielle's back. "At least Cadbury will be off your back for the moment."

"True. But we haven't got him off yours. Or Jareth's."

Not to mention the small issue of a wormhole out in space, doing who-knows-what.

Tristan sighs. "One step at a time, huh?"

Brielle smiles, the sweet motion unfurling something in his chest. "At least I have you captive in the meantime."

Chuckling, Tristan's hands tighten. "Can I be called a captive if I'm here willingly?"

Brielle giggles, her eyes flashing with delight. Knowing he put that glimmer there, it's the most captivating thing he's ever seen.

Suddenly, the air in the attic thickens as their smiles fade. Their lips gravitate to each other's and their breathing becomes shallow. Awareness detonates along Tristan's nerve endings. He wants this. He wants Brielle.

And there's nothing to hold him back from acting on those feelings. His gaze flickers to her mouth and Brielle draws in a sharp breath, her lips parting.

This kiss is full of passion. Heavy with desire. Hands start to move as they press closer, delve deeper. Tristan finds he's burning up and melting through and caving in all at once. When Brielle's hot fingers climb under his shirt, he moans. So does she.

Tristan's hands bunch at the hem of her top. He wants to feel her skin, too. Touch and taste and touch again.

Soulmate.

Tristan yanks back with a gasp. Brielle's mouth finds the point just below his ear, then roams lower, her tongue flicking to graze over the out-of-control pulse just below. The simple but sexy act has the word that just brushed though his mind evaporating.

But its impact doesn't. The cold brush of reality stains his mind.

Surprising even himself, Tristan does the opposite of what every shred of his being wants him to do. He pulls back.

"Frank and Bea might not be asleep, yet," he says huskily.

Brielle flushes. "I didn't wait as long as I normally would. I knew you'd be worried."

"I sure as hell appreciate my heart being started again," Tristan jokes. "But I don't want you to get in trouble if they find me up here."

Blinking, she nods. "Good thinking." She steps back. "I could come back later?"

Hating the shy note that's crept back into her voice, Tristan strokes a hand down her cheek. "You've had a big day. Maybe get some sleep?"

Brielle blinks again. "Sure. Also…good thinking."

She hesitates for a second, but Tristan stays where he is, gut clenched. She smiles a small smile. "I'll see you tomorrow."

Tristan gives her a jaunty salute. "I'll be here."

With a flutter of lashes and the slightest of frowns, she disappears back down the ladder.

What little smile he had fades the moment she's out of sight. That flicker of expression is part of the problem. Brielle and he are so in tune, and becoming more so every day, that she knows something's up. A moment later, the rectangle of light is extinguished.

Tristan sags as if the light was powering him, knowing full well it was Brielle's presence that truly lights him up. He walks back to his makeshift bed beside the window, acknowledging he won't be getting much sleep tonight.

The longer this goes, the more he wants. The more he realizes he can't do 'casual' with Brielle. What he feels for her is galaxies away from some friendly fling.

He sits down on the blankets, welcoming the hard floor beneath. Muted light soaks through the small window, drawing his gaze to the sky beyond it. The Universe he's supposed to be protecting is up there. There's a soulmate who was born at the exact same moment he was on the twin Gemini planet, waiting for him.

His head sinks into his hands as another question without an answer adds to the others.

How can something feel so right?

And yet be so impossible...

CASSANDRA

Butterflies flutter frantically inside Cassandra's belly as they get closer to her house. This is the second date she's had with Logan, and she's decided she's going to let him kiss her when he drops her off.

They turn a corner a block away from her house, and her heart races faster. With irritation, she realizes that she's nervous about kissing him for the first time. No guy has ever had this effect on her. She's used to being in control, using boys as playthings for her amusement. But Logan is no boy, and she likes him far more than any guy she's ever had a meaningless makeout session with when she was bored.

They pull up into her driveway, and the anxiety buzzing in her belly has spread through her extremities, making even her fingers tingle.

Stop being ridiculous, she chides herself in agitation.

She unbuckles her seatbelt and, to show she's in no hurry to get out, angles her body sexily to face him.

"Thank you for today," she purrs in a husky voice that usually makes guys melt. "I really enjoyed seeing your stomping grounds." Logan had taken her on a tour of his college campus in the city, and for dinner, they went to a restaurant across from Washington Square Park that was a popular hangout for the college crowd.

He smiles, and he looks so delicious in his just-snug-enough NYU t-shirt and blue jeans that she could eat him with a spoon. "Maybe I'll see you there next fall?"

"Maybe," she says with a playful shrug. "There are so many colleges that are desperately courting me. It's so hard to choose."

He shifts in his seat so that he's closer to her. "NYU would be lucky to have you."

He holds her gaze, and they just look at each other for a silent moment. She inches incrementally closer, puckering her lips ever so slightly, inviting him to close the distance. She hovers there, waiting.

And then he looks down at his lap.

The rejection is subtle but unmistakable, and Cassandra isn't sure whether to feel insulted or crushed.

Either way, she can't be in this confined space with him any longer, or the embarrassment is going to suffocate her.

"Goodnight, Logan." She pulls the handle and pushes open the door.

"Wait." His hand latches around her wrist, gentle but imploring.

She could pull away from his grip if she wanted to, but she allows it and turns to face him. His hand releases her wrist and slowly reaches up toward her face, hooking his index finger softly under her chin and pulling her closer.

He leans in, then hesitates, as if proceeding would break some unspoken rule. Is he afraid he'll scare her off by moving too quickly? Does he really imagine she's such a delicate flower?

His face is so close, she can feel his warmth, and the

desire to taste him is overwhelming. Unable to resist any longer, she closes the gap, pressing her lips to his.

For all the firmness of his muscled torso and arms, his lips are surprisingly soft. They give against hers like two silken pillows.

He sucks in a breath through his nose, as if the kiss causes him pain. But he doesn't recoil. Instead, his hand tangles into the hair at the base of her neck, pulling her closer as his lips part and close over hers.

His passion is sudden and intense as the strike of a match, and it ignites her own, her mouth opening in desperate invitation. His tongue greedily accepts, pushing into her mouth with a raw hunger that mirrors hers.

Lips and tongues push and pull at each other, devouring in a frenzied dance, a power struggle in which all are the victors, and submission tastes just as sweet as domination.

Logan is everything, filling every one of her senses. His hands roam, pressing and clutching, making her skin burn deliciously. His scent and taste commingle until they are one and the same, an intoxicating brew that tempts and satisfies at the same time. His harried breathing is like applause, cheering her on in her pursuit of him. And though her eyes are closed under passion-weighed lids, she can see nothing but what she wants to do to him, for him, with him.

Without conscious thought, she climbs over the center console and straddles his lap, reveling in the hardness of his body as she presses herself against him. His hands at her waist assist her, lifting her up and then pulling her down onto his lap.

She's never wanted anything or anyone this badly. It suddenly doesn't feel so bad to lose control, to give it over. With Logan, it feels right, a sweet surrender. And all she wants in this moment is him.

Her hands slide down his chest, eliciting a moan that can't

escape their tangled mouths. Her fingers find his jeans and tug at the button.

With a jolt, the same strong hands gripping her hips that pulled her closer suddenly push her away, yanking her mouth from his. They stare at each other for a moment, panting heavily. Her lips feel chapped, and confusion barges into her awareness, demolishing the desire that was so over-powering.

Logan shakes his head. "I... I can't do this." He lifts her off his lap, and feeling like a frightened turtle, she retreats across the stick shift, hugging herself.

"I-I'm sorry," she stammers softly, pleadingly. "I didn't mean to move so fast—"

"No, it's my mistake," he says, facing forward and focusing on catching his breath. "I'm sorry, I have to go."

Mistake.

What does he mean by that? Rejection seeps into her veins like a poison and spreads like wildfire until she feels sick with it.

She opens the door and steps out without another word.

"I'll call you," is all he says before he pulls the passenger door closed and drives away.

She stands on the lonely sidewalk for a moment after he's gone, trying to figure out what went wrong. Why did she reach for his pants? This was only their second date. Nice guys don't like to rush in, and Logan is a nice guy. The best guy. She might have just ruined everything.

Head hung low, she trudges up the driveway and into the house.

The inside is just as quiet as the outside. Her mother isn't home, and probably won't be until Cassandra's in bed. Ever since Cassandra's dark confession, her mother hasn't looked her in the eye, let alone stayed in a room with her long enough for a single word to be spoken. It appears that both of her parents are avoiding her now, and for the same ugly reason.

As she walks down the hall toward her room, she allows her mind to voice the thought she's been stifling for years: her family is a lie. Real fathers don't beat their daughters. Real mothers don't treat their daughters like dolls, toys to dress up and show off but show no affection to. Real families love each other, no matter what the flaws or mistakes. And she will never have a real family with her mom and dad.

But will she ever be able to stop loving them like they've stopped loving her?

The low hum of male voices catches her before she enters her room. She didn't think anyone was home, but it sounds like her dad is talking to someone in his office.

He actually decided to come home. Maybe he's finally done punishing me with his silence.

She pushes her bedroom door open, ready to curl up in bed and listen to music on her phone until she falls asleep.

"...happy that Brielle is out..." comes her dad's voice wafting down the hall.

At Brielle's name, Cassandra freezes. Why is her dad talking about Brielle? And to whom?

Curiosity tugs her toward his office like an invisible rope, and she peers in through the partially open door. Her dad is alone in the room, sitting in his swivel chair facing his computer. He's talking to someone via Skype.

"It was easy," says the man on the screen with a southern twang. From this angle, she can't see his face, just the back of her dad's head blocking the monitor. "The FBI really had no evidence to keep her there."

FBI?

Fright has Cassandra's hands inching toward the phone in her pocket to call Brielle, but she's glued to the spot so she doesn't miss any more golden nuggets of information.

"Let's hope it stays that way," her dad says.

"I'll make sure it does," replies the unknown man.

"Thank you, Solomon. You're an asset to our cause." And with that, the Skype window closes, the call terminated.

Her phone burning a hole in her pocket, Cassandra swiftly tiptoes to her room. She has to make sure Brielle is safe, and have two very important questions answered.

Who is Solomon?

And why is her father so interested in Brielle?

21

BRIELLE

Brielle picks at a loose string in the frayed knee of her jeans, winding and unwinding it around her index finger as the characters of *How I Met Your Mother* make the audience laugh on her laptop. Though she's seen every single episode a hundred times over the years when she lived at the orphanage, they are still a comfort to her whenever she is feeling down, and she's grateful for the ability to stream it without commercials.

It's definitely better than sitting in her room with nothing but silence to keep her company.

The events of the afternoon and evening have exhausted her energy, and she barely has any left to reflect on them.

Frank and Bea didn't seem the least bit suspicious about her run in with the FBI. And why should they? They truly believe that she's nothing but a sweet, normal girl. The drive home was full of consolations and apologies that she had to go through such ruthless interrogation. But they didn't ask questions, for which Brielle was very grateful. She wouldn't have lied to them. If they'd asked why the FBI thought Tristan and Jareth were involved with the asteroid explosion she would have answered honestly, damn the consequences. It's just too draining, too nerve-wracking, to be so secretive, especially to the people she cares about.

Instead, they just commented on how clueless government agencies were for suspecting a pair of teenagers for something that was obviously accomplished by a powerful and underground tech operation. Brielle just nodded silently to all of it. Better they build their own explanations.

And though the whole FBI thing had been harrowing, the part of the night that bothers her the most is the strange way Tristan pushed her away when she came back. He'd said it was just because he was worried that her parents would find them, but Brielle had sensed the lie, not that she even needed the use of her powers for that one. She just wishes she knew what his true reason was.

Her phone illuminates and begins to buzz on the side table. Mild curiosity as to who could be calling has her glancing at it.

Cassandra.

She probably just wants to chitchat. Brielle hasn't texted her about the day's events yet, but she'll have to if she answers, and she's too tired to go over the whole thing with Cassandra right now. Deciding she'll just tell Cassandra tomorrow at school, Brielle lets the phone go to voicemail.

Soon after the buzzing stops, a message lights up the screen that didn't even have time to fade to black.

With a sigh, Brielle picks up the phone and taps open the text.

Can you and Tristan stop playing house long enough to answer the phone? I really need to talk to you! Call me!

Brielle rolls her eyes at the insinuating comment and concedes, closing her laptop and pressing the phone to her ear.

"Thank you," Cassandra answers after one ring in that

snarky tone of hers. "When were you going to tell me that the FBI arrested you?"

Brielle frowns in surprise. "How did you find out?"

"I'll get to that. Are you okay?"

"Yes, I'm fine," Brielle answers, wondering if Tristan told her, and a twinge of jealousy jabs at her heart even as she knows it's foolish. "And they didn't arrest me, they just brought me in for questioning."

"That's hardly a difference," Cassandra scoffs. "What did they ask? What did you tell them?" Brielle can picture the determined fire in Cassandra's eyes, and she's grateful that it was her and not Cassandra who the FBI questioned.

Brielle's back sinks deeper into the pillow that's propping her up against the headboard. "They said Tristan and Jareth were suspected of involvement in the asteroid explosion and asked if I knew where they were hiding."

"Damn," Cassandra growls. "Please tell me you lied."

Brielle purses her lips. Cassandra must think she outed them. "I didn't have to. I answered with half-truths and redirected questions. And then some lawyer came in and insisted they release me."

"Was his name Solomon?"

Cassandra's question makes Brielle pause. "How did you know that?"

"That's the reason I called," Cassandra says with an excited lilt to her voice. "I overheard my dad skyping with someone just now, talking about you and the FBI. The guy's name was Solomon."

"Your dad?" Brielle exclaims, confusion constricting her voice into an alarmed squeal. "Why would your dad hire a lawyer to help me? And how did he even know the FBI brought me in?"

"I was hoping you would know," Cassandra replies, her

tone weighed down by disappointment. "Did your dad call him, maybe?"

"No, my dad said he didn't call anyone. He was just as surprised as I was when the lawyer showed up."

They sit quietly for a moment, their unspoken questions hanging in the amplified silence of the phone speaker.

"There's something else," Cassandra says slowly. "The way they were talking... It sounded like they knew more than they should."

"What do you mean?"

Cassandra makes a frustrated sound, then goes quiet, as if searching for the right words. "I can't really explain it. But there was one thing my dad said that I can't shake. He told Solomon that he was an asset to their cause."

This makes Brielle's heart thud. She tries to explain it away. "Maybe the cause is just keeping the company name clean?"

She can almost feel Cassandra's dubious frown. "Is that what you really think?"

"No," Brielle says with a sigh. That leaves one possibility glaringly open. "Do you...think he could be...working for Chardis?"

She expects Cassandra to immediately jump to her dad's defense and dismiss the idea.

"I don't know," Cassandra says instead. "But even so, why would Chardis care if you were busted by the FBI? One less target to worry about, right? This just—none of this makes any sense." She groans.

Brielle shakes her head. "I know."

"Are you really okay, though?" Cassandra asks in a gentler tone. "They didn't...hurt you or anything?"

"No, I'm fine," Brielle reassures.

"Did Tristan totally freak out?"

Brielle chortles. "He said he was ready to sneak out the window and go looking for me."

Cassandra gives a brief laugh. "I gotta say, I think it's super hot that you're hiding your boyfriend in your attic. There's something kinda Romeo and Juliet about it. How's the honeymoon going?"

Blush warms Brielle's cheeks, and again she's aware of Tristan's closeness, the fact that only one thin layer of wood separates them. Although after his strange withdrawal earlier, it feels like there's more getting in between them, something she can't yet see or define.

"I don't know." Brielle shrugs. "He was acting kinda weird tonight."

"It's Tristan," Cassandra says flatly. "Weird comes with the territory."

"I mean, he seemed distant," Brielle clarified.

"Well, put yourself in his shoes. He's on the run from the FBI, hiding in his girlfriend's attic. He has no freedom, and he's gotta feel cramped up there. And he's worried about you getting busted for hiding him. Give him a little slack. Hell, if he doesn't go completely insane and start talking to the walls, it'll be a surprise."

Brielle nods, still tugging at the loose string of her jeans. The hole at her knee is almost double the size. "I guess you have a point. I know this whole thing is really hard for him."

"Remember the positives," Cassandra says. "Tristan finally stopped being an idiot and agreed to date you. You got'im. You don't have to feel like you're still fighting for him."

But that's just it. Brielle is still fighting. And she may never stop. They both know he has a soulmate out there, a girl meant for him who *isn't her*. She's always going to feel like her time with Tristan is under threat, and she doesn't truly believe she'll be able to hand him over to another girl when this so-called soulmate shows up. She promised

Tristan casual, but she's not so sure she can do that. Maybe Tristan's distance was him trying not to get too close.

"You're right," Brielle says. "I have him for now." She can sense Cassandra getting ready to say something more on the subject, so she adds, "Today has been a really long day, and I gotta get up early. See you at school tomorrow?"

Cassandra sighs. "Sure. Just, try to enjoy what you've got. I'd kill to have a hot guy in my closet right now."

"Goodnight, Cassandra," Brielle chides before ending the call.

Why can't she be more like Cassandra? Kiss Tristan just for fun and not let her emotions get the better of her. But Brielle's a romantic. It's her curse. One of many, apparently.

She looks up at the ceiling, imagining Tristan laying on the floorboards above her. "Goodnight, Tristan."

She opens her laptop and taps the play button in the middle of her screen, hoping the familiar friendly voices will relax her to sleep. Maybe she'll be able to push away the thought that she wouldn't have to keep chasing Tristan if he would truly stop running.

22

VERONICA

Solomon Gray.

The name is embossed on a shiny metal plaque outside the mahogany door of his office.

Veronica bounces her foot, one leg crossed over the other, as she waits in the lobby for an audience with the mysterious lawyer. She hates these heels, and the rigid business skirt as well, but if she's going to interview for the position of receptionist at a legal firm, she needs to look the part. She already can't wait to let her hair out of its tight bun. Her thick dark locks were never meant for such confinement.

Her phone buzzes in the waist pocket of her suit jacket. She lifts it up enough to read the incoming message.

"I'm in position. Let me know when you're ready," reads Jareth's text.

She taps the thumbs up response to let him know she got it.

"Miss Styles?" calls a charming southern voice.

At the sound of her usual pseudonym, Veronica stuffs her phone deeper into the pocket and looks up, flashing Solomon Gray her perkiest smile. He stands in the open doorway, gesturing for her to come in with one hand and offering the other to shake.

She slips her hand into his coyly, doing her best impression of a wide-eyed doe ripe for slaughter. "Pleasure to meet you."

He guides her to his desk with his hand on her lower back —a bit too low—and she knows this will be easy. She takes the seat in front of his desk, doing a quick visual scan of the office for places to search as he moves to sit behind it. There's a rascally twinkle in his gray eyes as he smiles at her expectantly, and she's glad the skirt suit accentuates her curves so flatteringly.

"So, Miss Styles," he begins. "Why don't you tell me why you want to work for me?"

Veronica crosses her legs and rests her hands on her knee. "As you saw on my resume, I worked for the DA's office for several years, and frankly, there's not much money in that. I want to work for a real lawyer, one who doesn't have to worry whether or not his delinquent client is going to pay."

After her phone call with Logan last night, she immediately got to work researching the lawyer Logan told her about. Nothing came up except for a business listing and a job opening as a receptionist in his office in the city. What better way to meet this guy face-to-face and gain access to his office than apply for the job? Jareth helped her type up a fake resume that would look great to a guy like Solomon, and he called her first thing this morning to come in for an interview.

"Well, I'm flattered to know that I qualify as a real lawyer," he chuckles. "I used to work for the DA's office myself, so I can appreciate your desire to climb the ranks." He takes a look at the paper on the desk in front of him, and she recognizes her phony-baloney resume. "Who did you say referred you to me?"

"A friend of my mom mentioned you, said you got her daughter out of a legal spat the other day," she chances, and she knows it's a big risk. "A Miss Pierce." When the flash of suspicion crosses his face, she bats her eyes and cocks her head in a playful manner. "Britney or something, I think?"

Her feigned ignorance is accepted, and his expression returns to one of amused curiosity.

"You mean Brielle Pierce," he corrects with a nod.

"Yes, that was it!" Veronica exaggerates gratitude for the correction. "I know you have attorney-client privilege and all that, but I'm just so curious—what did the girl do? Allegedly." She throws in a wink.

He laughs, obviously thrilled by her candor. "Well, as you know, I can't discuss the details with you—"

"—unless you hire me," Veronica slips in.

He smiles. "But what I can say is that she is suspected of terrorist activity."

Veronica gasps. "Wow, really? Terrorists recruit young these days."

Solomon leans forward. "Apparently, so do lawyers. Pardon my frankness, but you look fresh outta high school, Miss Styles."

"Oh please, call me Viv," she implores.

Though his flirtation makes her want to gag—he's ancient, for pitch sake!—she's milking it for all it's worth. She needs to get information, preferably something she can share with her dad without further incriminating Brielle and the others. She'd avoid asking about Brielle at all, but from the brief texts she exchanged with her, Brielle doesn't know why he helped her, and since she's investigating this guy for her dad, she might as well help out her team at the same time.

"I don't know much about my mom's friend, but she doesn't seem like the type who can afford your services,"

Veronica baits. "Don't you typically represent wealthier clientele?"

His eyes darken, almost like a fog fills them. "Sometimes in life, we have to do things for bigger causes than money." His jaw sets, and she can tell he's not willing to share anything further on the topic.

"Achoo!" she squeals daintily, covering her nose. "Oh, excuse me. Do you have a tissues?"

"Of course." He reaches to the far end of his desk for the tissue box, and while he's not looking, she gingerly lifts up her phone and sends the message she'd typed earlier: "It's go time."

She replaces her hands on her lap just as he returns to face her with the box in hand. "Thank you." She takes a tissue and dabs at her nose.

Just then, there's a tap at the tall window to the parking lot. They both turn to see a handsome middle-aged man in a suit. Veronica recognizes him from their internet search last night—Richard Sinclair, Cassandra's adopted dad.

Solomon's face goes steely as Richard beckons him with the curl of his index finger.

"I'm so sorry, Miss St—Viv," Solomon says, not looking away from the window. "But I've got to step out for a moment. Would you mind waiting in the lobby?"

No. "Couldn't I just wait in here?" she asks sweetly, rubbing her arms. "It's just a bit chilly out there..."

"Of course," he says, then gets up and heads out the door.

Leaving her alone in his office.

Perfect. Just according to plan.

She waits until she sees Solomon talking to Richard through the blinds before she swings around the desk to snoop. Opening the filing cabinet, she scans the names until she sees Brielle Pierce. She yanks out the file and speed reads it. But there's nothing of value on it, just her basic profile information, stuff Veronica, and no doubt her dad and the FBI, already know.

Closing it and putting it back neatly into place, she shuts the cabinet and resorts to searching his desktop. Solomon clearly doesn't expect anyone to get on except him, because he leaves all his accounts open. She takes a quick peruse through his emails, his Facebook, every open tab there is. His Facebook is a snore-fest, no messages, and his Instagram is surprisingly nothing but non-stop animal friends pictures. This guy has a shocking affinity for cute penguin-cat friendships.

Weird.

Coming up short, she riffles through his computer files. Woah! Some of his clients are serious psychos! There are crime scene photos that make her stomach turn and have her closing them instantly. No more pictures. She realizes that much of this, though not related to the Zodiacs, would still help out the FBI quite a bit. Which might be perfect, as she doesn't actually want to incriminate her friends.

She pulls a flash drive out of her other breast pocket and inserts it, quickly dragging as much as she can into the empty folder. She glances at the window. Solomon is saying goodbye to Richard-slash-Jareth!

Crap! Hurry up, hurry up, hurry up!

The last file loads and she yanks out the drive and rushes back to her seat on the other side. Just as she regains her composure, Solomon saunters through the door.

"Sorry about that, Viv," he says, his southern drawl in full charm mode. "Some of these clients, as you will learn, can be quite demanding."

"So does that mean I have the job?" she asks, more for her ego than anything else.

"I think your chances are very good," he replies as he reclaims his seat and rests his ankle on his knee. "I have to meet with a few of the other applicants, you understand, but you're definitely the one to beat."

She smiles her most toothy smile. "Then I look forward to hearing from you. Unfortunately, I have to run."

"Oh?" He sounds disappointed, and she smooths her skirt as she stands.

"Have a good evening," she says, and sashays out of his office.

She walks down the sidewalk that hugs the parking lot, continuing her sashay until she rounds the corner just in case Solomon is still watching. As soon she turns past the bushes, Richard emerges, shedding his illusion as he approaches and becoming her beloved Jareth once again.

"Definitely an improvement," she greets, opening her arms to hug him.

"Did you find anything?" he asks, his energy very hyped. She imagines it would after pretending to be someone he's never met. Her heart twinges as she realizes how grateful she is to have someone to perform these hoodwinks with. She's never had a partner like this.

Her dad really has no idea how talented an asset she could be if he just let her in.

"Nothing on the Zodiacs, which is good but not good," she says with a frown. "But I did get lots of dirt on various other criminals that my dad will hopefully like."

Jareth starts speaking before she finishes, full of an excitement that seeps into her by osmosis. "Well, you won't believe what he told me!"

Aching with intrigue, she asks, "What?"

"He told me they know there's another Zodiac!"

"What!" she shrieks. She shakes her head. "How does Cassandra's dad know about Zodiacs?"

He looks from side to side, hushing his voice. "I don't know, but somehow, he's involved. All I know is, I asked him about Brielle, and he said, 'Everything is taken care of. And we're getting close to the next heir, but every time we approach, the others come in.'"

She shakes her head, overwhelmed with information at the moment. "Wait, so they're getting close to finding the next heir? Before us?"

He nods avidly. "And apparently, we've run into whoever it is, multiple times."

Mind. Blown.

"Holy crap! We have to tell the others!" she peeps.

"There's something else," he says, voice even more hushed. "He let on that they can sense when we use our powers. That's how they tracked down this new heir."

They share a long, exhaustive look.

"Ah, pitch."

23

LOGAN

Logan feels like his life is on repeat. Keep tabs on Cassandra. Give in to the undeniable draw and see her, pretending he needs to gain more information.

Fall even more deeply into the mess he's making of this.

And then lie to his father, reassuring him he's getting close.

Getting close isn't the problem…

Logan shoves away the half-eaten pizza, adding the box to the pile on the driver's side seat. And yet, he's here again, sitting outside Cassandra's house on a stake out, about to do it all again.

What the hell is wrong with him?

Glancing at the clock on his dashboard, he notes it's just after seven. Night descended a little while ago, cloaking him in darkness as if the world is trying to hide his shame. His father's voice climbs through his mind thanks to the phone call they just had.

We need answers, Logan.

He needs to tell him. Right now, he's no better than Veronica…

There's a movement in one of the upstairs windows—
Cassandra's room. Images of her sitting on her bed, probably
in a tank top and low riding pajama pants unwillingly climb
into Logan's consciousness. The sensation of her skin
grazing over his fingertips has them tingling all over again.

Since when did kisses burn you from the inside out?

He sighs loudly. Since when was he reduced to acting like
a hormone driven teen?

Logan grabs the can of soda in the drink holder and
drains it. It's just that Cassandra's so...*hot!*

There's a fire that burns inside her, a fire that makes her
strong and sassy, sexy and sultry, spirited and surprising. He
can't get enough of it.

He crushes the can, liking the feeling of it crumpling in
his palm. Maybe it's her alien powers doing this. It certainly
feels like he's under some sort of spell. As if all reason has
been scorched from his mind.

His eyes widen. Is that it? Is she using some sort of mind
power? Some sort of emotion manipulation? Logan
straightens in his seat. That explains everything! How else
could one kiss explode into lap-climbing, skin-seeking
passion? Heck, they were about to go all the way, right in this
same spot! Outside her house!

Grabbing his phone, Logan frowns as he opens their chat.
He can't believe he didn't figure this out sooner. What a fool
he's been!

His cheeks flaming with shame, Logan types. He's never
going to tell his father about this. Jack Cadbury doesn't need
to know how easily his son was almost turned against him.

Hey, watcha up to?

There's a pause, one much longer than usual. Logan
glances at the window, noting that a light doesn't come on.
Maybe Cassandra's asleep?

His phone dings. *Just hanging.*

Logan chews his lip. He knows he acted weird—again—after their explosive make out session, so he's not surprised she's keeping it cool.

He frowns. Except, she's probably an alien.

Me, too. We should 'just hang' together…

Sounds like a 'mistake' to me.

Logan blinks, not liking the sense of hurt that permeates through the phone and climbs into his chest. He tightens his hold on it.

She's the one manipulating him.

I freaked out a bit, sorry. I've never felt anything like that. His cheeks flush at the truth behind those words.

He pauses, then quickly types again.

I want to see you again. The sooner the better. Maybe tonight?

He knows he's being forward, but Logan presses send, anyway. If Cassandra really is an alien trying to use him, then this is exactly what she wants.

Sorry, can't tonight. I'm off to bed as I have a track meet early tomorrow morning.

The frown is back as Logan wonders what that means. Is she taking this game to the next level and playing hard to get? He quickly types a reply.

Sure, maybe another time. I'm not giving up ;P

There's no answer, which is even more confusing.

Silence descends in his pizza-infused car once again, and Logan is left with nothing but his thoughts.

Either Cassandra is an alien, and he's betraying the man who adopted him as his own.

Or she's not, and he's sabotaging something just as extraordinary and out of this world.

He rests his head back against the seat, realizing he should've brought something caffeinated.

The next few hours are going to be exhausting as he

jumps back on this mental rollercoaster. One that never reaches an end.

He's just dozing off when a movement at the side of the house wakes him. He stills, watching a lithe, curvy figure that could only be Cassandra slip into the garage. A moment later, her car pulls out, the headlights off as she rolls down the driveway.

Glancing at the clock, Logan notes it's almost midnight. So much for an early night…

He follows at a distance, and it only takes a few turns to realize she's going to Tristan's house.

Once he knows the destination, Logan allows himself to fall even further back. He drums his fingers on the steering wheel in thought. Cassandra hasn't demonstrated any links to Ayers since the spotlight fell squarely on the slippery troublemaker. It's the only shred of evidence that's allowed Logan to believe maybe the burn marks on the table were just a freak coincidence.

But she's most definitely heading to Tristan's house. In the middle of the night.

After blowing Logan off.

He watches from the end of the street as Cassandra pulls up out the front of the large house. There are no other cars around, but he doubts she's here alone.

Is this some kind of tryst?

Hating the jealousy that stings through his veins, Logan slips lower in his seat as Cassandra climbs out of her car. Her blonde hair catches the street light as she glances over her shoulder, first one way, then the other. Even from here, Logan can sense the tightness that's wound through her. She's on high alert.

To his surprise, she doesn't go to the front door, instead walking around and heading down the side. Logan checked this place out enough times to know there's an eight-foot high concrete wall surrounding the backyard, like some cultish compound. There's no gate—also interesting—which has him even more curious as to what Cassandra's up to.

The jealousy flares again, this time hotter and sharper, making it harder to ignore.

She's meeting someone. But who?

With another furtive glance over her shoulder, Cassandra disappears into the night engulfing the house. Frowning, Logan calls his dad, only to find it goes straight to voicemail. The frown deepening, Logan knows he has a decision to make.

Not giving himself time to change his mind, he sends two quick texts. Then, he leaves his car and follows her.

Light-footed and avoiding the pools of light the street casts periodically, he tries to be as invisible as possible. With limited visibility, and Cassandra too far ahead to be heard, Logan turns inward to keep tabs on her.

If she hears him, he'll sense it.

But there are no startled tugs on her consciousness, no jolts of fear. Just the tense, edgy hold on her emotions.

The Ayers house is situated at the edge of suburbia, sparse woodland surrounding the rear of the house. As Logan blends among the trees, he notes how secluded it feels. He grinds his teeth so hard he has to stop before something cracks. The perfect place for a secret hook up.

He walks further into the trees, creating more distance from the house. He needs to be close enough to see what's going on, but far away enough that he won't be easily discovered. Resting his back against the rough bark of a tree, he prepares to wait. Taking his night vision goggles out of his pocket, he slips them on.

The world is cast in eerie shades of green as Cassandra's slender form appears near the wall of the compound. She checks her phone, the screen flashing white, only to quickly tuck it away again. Crossing her arms, she leans against the concrete expanse she's remained close to.

A few more minutes pass and Logan senses she's getting impatient. She'd probably be pacing if she wasn't trying to be so invisible.

Logan chews his lip as he waits with her. As the unwanted jealousy, disgustingly underscored by hurt, tries to take over, he reminds himself of several glaring truths.

She's an alien who's been manipulating his emotions. One who's a danger to Earth.

Or, she's an alien who's been seeing someone else the whole time she was stringing him along.

And is still a danger to Earth.

Or she's human...and she's been seeing someone else the whole time she was stringing him along.

In each and every scenario, Logan's the chump. And his father hasn't been vindicated.

Suddenly, Cassandra pushes away from the wall. Logan straightens too, still and taut as he waits to see what she's heard.

Surprisingly, Cassandra looks up, and Logan tenses even more as he feels alarm jolt through her.

His breath whooshes out when he sees what she must be seeing.

Two figures are descending through the branches. Two suited figures. And they're flying.

They land feet first, one male and one female judging by the curves and angles of their outlines. There's no way to see the color of the armor covering them, but Logan knows it's them.

The Zodiacs.

The ones who destroyed the asteroid.

He lifts his phone, his body moving on autopilot. Every hour of training has come down to this moment. Pointing it in their direction, he takes a photo, his eyes impossibly widening even more.

As his thumb presses the button, the suits retract. Simply disappear.

And leave Tristan and Brielle standing in their place.

Logan's knees go weak as he's faced with irrevocable proof that his father is right. Tristan is an alien. So is Brielle.

And Cassandra is with them, definitely not looking like Logan is feeling—as if her entire understanding of the world just imploded.

Tristan jerks to attention, his posture unerringly turning toward where Logan is standing several yards away. "Did you see that?"

The camera flash. Logan was too shocked to think of turning it off. He's been discovered.

There's a subtle crunching of leaves behind him and he realizes it doesn't matter. The backup he texted for has arrived. His father obviously hasn't seen the one Logan also sent him. More men than he would've expected morph around him, faces impassive as they hone in on the three figures.

"It's them," Logan chokes out before turning away.

As the agents move in, he stumbles backward. A second later he's running, sprinting, almost as if he's desperately trying to leave the truth behind.

But he can't.

He has undeniable evidence. Photographic proof.

And he has to show his father.

24

TRISTAN

Before Tristan can jolt into action and find out what the flash of light was, a voice erupts from the trees.

"Freeze, you're under arrest!"

Pitch! How did the feds find them?

Tristan grabs Brielle's hand. "Follow me!"

He breaks into a sprint and heads straight for the trees behind the walled yard. He's not surprised to find Cassandra right beside him, showing no difficulty in keeping up.

Tristan doubts she guessed all those years of track training would be used to run from the law.

"Shouldn't we be running *toward* the house?" Cassandra demands between breaths.

Tristan glances over his shoulder, noting about seven dark forms several yards behind them. "And just increase the surveillance on it?"

"Then where are we going?" Brielle pants.

"You'll see."

There's no way he's blurting what he discovered out loud. Not when they could be overheard.

Tristan shoves a branch out of the way, tugging on

Brielle's hand, the sound of multiple feet storming through the woods behind them making his heart thump. They can't use their suits or their powers. It's too risky.

As much as he hates it, evasion is their best bet.

"We need to create some distance between us," he tells the other two.

Cassandra lengthens her stride. "You'll need to keep up then."

She streaks forward, and Tristan grunts with respect. No fed is going to be able to keep up with her.

But he can hear Brielle's labored breathing. She hasn't endured the training that Cassandra and he have.

There's a *crack* and something *zings* past Tristan's head. He instinctively ducks, drawing Brielle closer to him as he registers what that was. A gunshot.

They're shooting at them?

"Suits!" Tristan calls out.

There's a trio of "Akashs" whispered and Tristan is engulfed, just like Cassandra and Brielle are.

"I thought they'd want us alive," gasps Brielle through their coms.

"Which means they're not FBI," mutters Tristan.

They're being chased by Skins.

As if to prove his theory, one of the men breaks free of the group, closing the distance between them. No fed could run that fast. Only a soulless killing machine infused with dark matter could inject that much speed.

Brielle's breathing is even louder through their shared communication. It's only a matter of time before a Skin catches up.

Zarius's voice whispers through Tristan's mind. *Use your surroundings to your advantage.*

He releases Brielle's hand. "Keep running due south."

"But—"

Tristan leaps before she can finish her sentence. He grabs a thick branch above them and yanks, wood cracking and splintering as he tears it off the trunk. Brielle must realize what he's doing because she darts ahead, leaving him room for what he's about to execute.

Spinning around, Tristan lowers his arms as if he's doing a bench press. Except this isn't some five-hundred-pound barbell. It's a chunk of tree. He squats and throws it with all his might, a little awed as he watches it sail through the air. His suit sure as pitch amplifies his strength!

It hits the first Skin and knocks him over like a bowling pin, never losing momentum as it crashes into the next ones. Tristan doesn't wait to see what destruction he just wrought, instead breaking into a run again.

"We're getting close," he tells the others through their coms as he tries to catch up. Injecting a blast or two between each step, he zips between the trees as if gravity was just halved.

"Close to what?" Cassandra asks, sounding exasperated.

Tristan reaches Brielle first. No doubt she slowed down so he could reach her. His heart swells as he brushes his hand over hers. It's a brief touch, barely a caress, but it's enough.

They're in this together in a way they never have been before.

Tristan stops, knowing he's probably only bought them a few minutes. He needs to find it. ASAP.

Although his suit allows him to see in the dark in ways he doubts even the military can, all the trees look the same. When he memorized the location, he thought he'd have more time to find it when they met tonight.

But Skins are on their tails. Skins with guns.

Tristan spins around, frantically scanning left and right.

"What are you looking for?" Brielle asks. "Maybe we can help."

"A tree," he mutters, more to himself than anything. "With the branches crossed like an X."

Cassandra hikes her hands on her hips. "You've got to be kidding me. That could be anywhere!"

But Brielle is already looking, scanning the canopy around them. She points to one a few feet away. "Like that one?"

Tristan's eyes widen and his visuals intuitively zoom in on where she's pointing. "Yes!"

Two branches high above crisscross forming a perfect letter X.

He rushes forward. "It seems Alden liked cliches." Squatting down beside the trunk, he feels for the metal latch. "Got it!" He lifts a hatch, shiny metal underneath, leaf litter camouflage on top. "X marks the spot," he announces triumphantly.

Cassandra strides over, staring into the tunnel now gaping back at her. "No way."

Brielle joins her. "Alden, you genius," she breathes.

Exactly what Tristan says on a regular basis. He beckons them to get in. "Quick, we need to disappear."

Cassandra clambers down the ladder with Brielle behind her. Tristan follows them, closing the hatch after them and locking it. He grasps Brielle's hand again, leading her down the tunnel. Although it's black as night in here, their suits mean they can see everything.

"I found another entrance to HQ when I was looking around the other night," Tristan explains as he walks. "My guess is Alden installed it so we have an exit if the house has been compromised. Right now, it's a safer way to enter. "

"Yep, that man is a genius," Brielle says in awe.

Shelves begin to appear, lining the tunnel, telling Tristan

they're getting close to the central room. Doors dot either side, some rooms still full of technology he's yet to figure out. He ignores it all for now.

They need to know whether they've gotten away.

Inside HQ, Tristan retracts his suit, and Brielle and Cassandra do the same. He scans the images on the screens, searching for the cameras aimed along the concrete wall. The last one shows him the image he's looking for.

"I always used to wonder why Alden had this aimed at a random section of the forest."

Brielle leans in close. "For the hatch!"

Tristan enlarges the video stream on the big screen, showing several fed-Skins in the area. Whatever technology is inside the suits that allows them to see in darkness has obviously been installed in the surveillance cameras. The images beyond the walls are almost as crisp and clear as day.

"They've disappeared!" one of the Skins mutters in frustration, the words reaching them through the speakers.

"The fools have flown off. NASA would be scanning for a bunch of suits up there. We just need to wait for them to get caught."

One of the other men growls. "There's a body we need to clean up."

Probably the first Skin bowled over by the branch.

"We deal with that," the first one answers. "Then, we wait until these FBI fools give us another tip off."

The men disperse, disappearing from view.

Cassandra lets out a long breath. "That was close."

"Too close," says Tristan. His gaze flicks over the screens until he finds the right one. He's not going to allow himself to relax until he knows how they were found.

Expanding the camera that focuses on the backyard wall, Tristan starts to search through the footage.

"What are you looking for?" Cassandra asks.

Tristan's cell rings before he can answer. He registers the caller on the screen. "Hey, you're late."

"Sorry," Jareth says, not sounding it. "We thought we had a tail so took the long way here."

"Good thinking. You missed all the fun, though. Some Skins found us."

"Disappointing," Jareth says dryly. "What happened?"

Tristan frowns as something flickers on the images rewinding on the screen. He hits pause. "I'll get Cassandra to let you in. She can get you up to speed. She'll meet you at the wall, like we agreed."

Cassandra nods before breaking into a jog, disappearing into the tunnel at the other end of the room.

Brielle steps forward, placing a hand on Tristan's shoulder. "Are you okay?"

He pauses, surprised at the question. And touched. "Hopefully."

Her green eyes study him, perceptive as always. "You think we shouldn't have flown."

Tristan sighs, no longer questioning how Brielle can practically read his mind. "No, we shouldn't have. It was a foolish risk."

No matter how amazing it is to cruise through the skies with this girl at his side. He's pretty certain that was a camera flash that caught his attention, even as he desperately hopes it wasn't.

"If we came here by car, we probably would've been followed," Brielle points out. "You may be impulsive, Tristan, but you don't take foolish risks."

Tristan loses the ability to move for long seconds as Brielle's words wash over him. A feeling he hasn't felt for a long time blooms deep within his chest.

Comfort.

"Thanks," he says huskily.

Brielle wrinkles her nose at him. "Anytime."

One word whispers through Tristan. *Forever.*

He clears his throat before he allows himself to acknowledge it. Straightening in his chair, he turns back to the screen. "Let's hope it's all okay, then."

Tristan presses play and the flash of light he saw flickers brightly. Pausing it, he rewinds, and clicks play again. This time, he zooms in on the location of the flash.

A figure fills the image. A guy. Most definitely holding a cell phone. In slow motion, the flash erupts from the device, flares bright and recedes again.

No doubt capturing Tristan and Brielle mid-flight.

Brielle gasps. "I've seen him before."

"You have? Where?"

"Weeks ago. He was parked at our driveway. He drove off before I could ask any questions."

Which means this douche has been following them for some time. "We need to find out who he is. I guarantee he called the Skins on us."

Brielle's face tightens. "Which means he's a Skin, too."

The sounds of footsteps echo through HQ and Cassandra appears with Jareth and Veronica.

Cassandra turns her smiling face to them. "Who's a Skin?"

Her gaze travels to the screen on the wall and she freezes. Her eyes widen as her mouth pops open. "It can't be…"

But before Tristan can ask how she just recognized the guy, Veronica gasps and her hand flies to her mouth.

"Logan!"

Standing, Tristan looks from the two shocked female faces back to the frozen image on the screen. "Who's Logan?"

Veronica's eyelids flutter, but it doesn't stop the moisture pooling along them. "That's no Skin, Tristan." Her face crumples and she grips Jareth's hand. "That's my brother."

Tristan almost reels back with shock. Jack Cadbury's son?

Cassandra collapses into the nearest chair, her face pale. "And the guy I've been seeing," she says weakly.

Suddenly, Tristan wants to do the same. He locks his knees because his muscles suddenly feel like custard. "He took a photo of us. He has proof."

And right now, he's taking it straight back to the FBI.

25

CASSANDRA

The shock is almost too much to bear. The sight of Logan's face on the screen reverberates a shockwave through Cassandra, almost like an earthquake only she can feel, and in its wake, all that's left is a numbness.

But only at first.

That tingly nothingness is only a buffer, her nervous system's defense from the true pain it refuses to process.

Logan.

How could it be? How could he turn out to be a spy for the FBI? The way she feels about him… That kind of connection, that spark, isn't something that can be manufactured. No one has ever made her feel the way he did, like she was invincible and vulnerable at the same time.

And it was all a lie?

Cassandra's hands clench, her palms heating as the numbness fractures. Men don't get to do this to her. Not after she discovered who she really is. Not after she put her dad in his place. She swore to never let anyone hurt her again, especially a man. She's not just some blonde bimbo guys can manipulate. She's the Leo Guardian, dammit! A force to be reckoned with.

"Wait, what do you mean you've been seeing him?" Brielle's green gaze is confused under furrowed brows. "You never mentioned a new guy..."

Cassandra shakes her head, not letting a single ounce of the pain or anger she feels cross her face. She won't give Logan any more power to influence her. "It was too early. I just met him a few days ago, and with everything going on with you guys, me meeting a guy didn't seem like terribly important news."

Despite the light, flippant way Cassandra speaks about him, Brielle's frown deepens, like she can see right through Cassandra's skin to her bleeding heart.

Brielle pulls a chair close and sits in front of Cassandra, placing a comforting hand on her lap. "I'm sorry."

Cassandra shrugs and rolls her eyes, her gaze falling on Veronica when the eye-roll completes. White hot fury splashes up out of the pit of molten heartache in her gut like a solar flare. "What is it with your family and tricking people into liking you? First you get your hooks into Jareth, and now your brother tries to woo me? Are you still on their side? Are you still a spy?" Her voice is echoing through HQ when she finishes, almost shouting the accusation.

Jareth immediately slips in between her and his girl-friend, and Veronica clutches his shirt, shaking her head at him imploringly.

"I wouldn't—" she starts to say.

"I know," he cuts her off softly, then turns to Cassandra. "Whatever her brother did, Veronica isn't like that. She ran away from Jack when she found out he was sending the feds after me."

"Maybe that's just what she wants you to think," Cassandra hisses, tasting the poison in her voice. She needs to hurt someone, and since Logan isn't here, his sister is the next best thing.

Tristan shifts in his chair, crossing his arms and regarding them all with a calculating expression. "Veronica didn't know about her brother...right?" He looks to Veronica for verification.

A sick sort of satisfaction coils in Cassandra's belly at the fact that she's brought Tristan to doubt. Her palms itch with familiar fire, and the desire to blow something up is overwhelming. But she'll have to settle for social destruction for now. These quarters are too tight for the release she craves.

"Guys, I swear I had no idea Logan was even talking to Cassandra," Veronica vows, back straightening defensively as she stands. Jareth's hand tightens around hers, holding fast at her side.

It makes Cassandra's heart twist with disgust.

"Veronica isn't lying to us, Cassandra," Brielle insists, her eyes full of conviction. "If she was, I would have sensed it. We can't start turning on each other, especially not now."

"Right," Tristan says with a strained sigh. "Because whatever evidence they had on us before, they now have irrefutable proof. And it's not just Jareth and me in the hot seat anymore. It's you girls, too."

The fire in Cassandra's chest that Brielle's words had started to quell only rages hotter at Tristan's.

Cassandra jerks her head away from Veronica, hating her if only for the simple reason that she's the sister of the guy who... The first guy she...

She blinks away the hot tears that threaten, keeping her head down so no one sees. "What are we going to do?" she practically growls.

"None of our homes are safe now." Tristan kicks at the leg of his chair, eyes darting between Brielle and Cassandra. "They'll go to both of your houses looking for all of us."

Brielle's face blanches at that, and Cassandra knows the horror Brielle must be feeling. She just got a family, a real one, after so long of waiting and hoping for one. Now she's going to lose them forever.

"We could go to the orphanage," Veronica suggests. "Sister Agatha has been very gracious about letting us stay."

Jareth shakes his head. "She just thinks she's sheltering a runaway and an ex-orphan who've come on hard times. If all five of us take refuge there, she'll suspect something, and people will talk. I'm honestly surprised the feds haven't come by to ask about any of us already."

"Then we'll do like I'd originally planned," Tristan says. "We go on the run. Only this time, we'll all stay together." Cassandra doesn't miss the way his eyes flicker to Brielle, the way the corners of his lips twitch upward when their eyes meet.

Right now, it just makes her sick.

Maybe love isn't real. All this time, she thought her parents loved her. But her dad just wants to mold her into his idea of the perfect girl and beat her if she falls short. And her mom, well, that woman only loves herself.

Maybe love is just a lie people use to hurt you and get what they want from you. Veronica did it to Jareth. Logan did it to her. And Tristan and Brielle are doing it to each other, they just don't realize it yet.

It's all a bunch of bullshit.

"Not before I get some answers," Cassandra grumbles behind clenched teeth. "I'm calling him." She gets off the chair and storms down the hall, tapping Logan's name on her phone.

She paces back and forth, like a lioness on the prowl, listening to steady ringing and waiting for her chance to pounce.

But he doesn't answer. The call goes to voicemail, and she

hates how the sound of his recorded voice asking her to leave a message still makes her heart twinge.

In a fit of fury, she pelts her phone against the wall, the sudden absence of its light and the echoing clatter telling her she's shattered it into pieces.

He doesn't get to ignore her like this. He's going to answer for his betrayal.

She glances at her friends, huddled in debate of where they should flee to, what they should grab, when they should make their escape. None of them are paying any attention to her. Cassandra's just throwing a tantrum again, they must be thinking. No one cares about her pain.

Even as the thoughts cross her mind, she knows she's being petty, but the hurt is writhing inside her, the hot lava boiling up and splashing at her insides.

She has to be her own hero, and if she's forced to go into hiding, she'll be damned if she does so without making Logan face her.

Taking advantage of being in the blind spot of her friends, she sneaks further down the tunnel and out the secret hatch.

This won't be like the last time she went rogue. There's nothing left to expose. The cat's already out of the bag— because of Logan. And this kitty is going to show him her claws.

Once she's made him pay for crossing her, she'll be back in a snap, and maybe her friends will be safer for it.

BRIELLE

"So, what's the plan?"

Though it was Jareth who said the words, it's the question that's on each of their minds.

Tristan rubs his hands down his face. "We grab as many essentials as we can from here and hop on the next train out of town. Go to some place far away, a town small enough that it won't have a large FBI presence but not small enough that every resident will know our names."

Brielle wonders if that formula was how Zarius had kept them moving. But then, the FBI wasn't actively on their tail when Tristan was growing up. Back then, his family only moved from place to place to find other Zodiacs.

They weren't on the run.

"But what about the other Zodiac?" Jareth asks. That was the reason they called this meeting. "The Skins are close to finding him or her. How can we leave?"

Tristan purses his lips grudgingly. "We'll figure something out. We just have to get somewhere safe, somewhere off the feds' radar. We're no good to this new Zodiac as wanted criminals."

Jareth and Veronica nod.

The whole thing makes Brielle sick to her stomach. She'll be wanted for terrorism. She can flush away any hopes of having the normal life she always dreamed of all those years in the orphanage. She'll never graduate high school, never go to college and get a good job...never marry a nice man and start a family...

She can't help but steal a glance at Tristan as she thinks this. At the moment, her best—and possibly only ever—romantic prospect is a guy who's only staying with her until the next girl comes along.

Tristan's eyes meet hers and she instinctively looks away.

That's not even the worst part. The most painful thing about all of this is that she'll now have to throw away the wonderful, amazing and loving parents she's only had for a few weeks, and she can't even say goodbye. Any minute now, the FBI will go to her house looking for her and tell Frank and Bea who and what she is. Whatever love and trust they may have begun to develop for her will shrivel like a wilted sprout, never to know its full potential.

Brielle clutches her throat, fighting back the bile that rises.

"We'll go into the house and pack some supplies," Veronica volunteers, and she and Jareth slip out of HQ.

Tristan looks around at all the tech on the walls. All the stuff they're going to have to leave behind.

"What are we going to do about all this?" she asks, her voice so soft she barely recognizes the sound. She clears her throat, but the acid lingers like a bad aftertaste. "We still don't know anything about the wormhole. How will we ever destroy it without being able to monitor it? There's no way we can take all this with us."

Tristan nods. "The best we can do is backup as much as possible onto a portable drive and take it with us."

"How long will that take?"

Tristan frowns with a shrug. His movements have much less umph, and Brielle can tell this turn of events has taken a heavy toll on him, too. "An hour, maybe two. In fact, I'd better get started." He turns to face the computers and begins tapping away.

"Is there anything I can do?" She hopes he hears the deeper meaning in the question.

"You can pack the gems and nanites for me," he suggests. "Those are our most valuable possessions, so handle them with care."

"I will." She nods meaningfully. Then she looks behind her. "Cassandra?"

But Cassandra isn't there. Wasn't she just here a second ago?

"Oh no," Brielle groans.

Tristan turns concerned eyes to her. "What's wrong?"

The bile threatens again. "Cassandra's gone."

Tristan grunts. "Not again!"

With anxiously trembling fingers, Brielle pulls out her phone and dials Cassandra. The phone goes instantly to voicemail. Every muscle in Brielle's body tightens with angst.

"Her cell is turned off," she grouses, her pulse quickening as worry-fueled images fill her mind. "Should I go after her?"

Tristan shakes his head, huffing in frustration. "We don't even know where she went. If you go searching for her, you could get caught by the feds."

"But what if she gets caught?" Brielle can barely manage to get the words out.

He rakes his fingers through his hair, then rests his head on his hand halfway through, considering. "Well, I mean, let's face it. The girl's a walking supernova. If she does get caught, she won't stay that way for long. I don't think it's so much

Cassandra's safety we have to worry about, just what trouble she'll cause."

Brielle closes her eyes, trying not to dwell on the worrisome scenarios that play in her mind. "She did just have her heart broken. Maybe she just needed some air and will come back soon."

Tristan nods, though she can tell he doesn't put much stock in that possibility.

Neither does she. If Cassandra was just going for a walk, she wouldn't have turned off her phone.

Brielle's known Cassandra her whole life, and in all that time, Cassandra had never really liked a guy. She'd strung a few along, toyed with them, but none of them ever really got close. She wouldn't let them. Though Brielle didn't know anything about this new guy before a few minutes ago, and though Cassandra said she'd only just met him, Brielle could tell by the simmering anger in Cassandra's amber eyes that she'd let this one in.

And he betrayed her.

The only guy she'd ever opened her heart to just smashed it into a million pieces.

Cassandra has to be pissed. And hell hath no fury like Cassandra, especially a broken-hearted Cassandra.

If Brielle knows her like she thinks she does, her bet is that Cassandra went to find Veronica's brother.

Pitch, I hope I'm wrong.

"Any chance you're getting a vision that might tell us where she is?" she asks, trying to sound lighthearted but it just comes out sounding nervous.

"Not at the moment," he says with a dry laugh. "I always hate it when they come, hate how powerful they are and the warnings they give. But..." He chews his cheek. "When I really need to know something, need answers, they're as silent as the grave. Sometimes, I wish I could control them, conjure them at will to show me the possible outcomes of any choice." His eyes slowly creep up to look at her, and she senses he's not just talking about locating their trigger-happy friend.

He's wondering if he made the right choice in dating her.

She doesn't want to get into that, especially right now. She steers the conversation in another direction. "It seems to me that you only get your visions when something terrible is about to happen. Right?"

He nods once. "Yeah, I guess. I've never had a vision about something mundane, like going to school or eating breakfast."

A small spark of relief ignites in her chest, and she wills it to spread. "Then maybe the fact that you're not having a vision about Cassandra right now means she'll be fine."

The wrinkles in his forehead smooth and he sits up straighter. His lips even begin to spread into a small smile, and he reaches out for her. "I love how you always look at the glass as half full."

She gives him her hand, and he pulls her closer. His palm is warm, comforting, and suddenly she's not so afraid. Yes, she loves Frank and Bea so much for taking her in and showing her what having a family could be like. But she'd let herself forget that Jareth, Cassandra, and Tristan...are her true family. And she's so grateful to have Tristan right now.

"I'm sorry about this, about..." He stops, but she knows what he was going to say.

"I know." She sighs. "But there's nothing we can really do but roll with the punches, right?" She forces her lips to spread, and she finds that, under Tristan's gentle gaze, his hand holding hers, her mouth wants to smile.

Her mouth wants to do more than that.

And like they're on the same wavelength, Tristan rises from his swivel chair and takes her in his arms.

His lips cover hers. Hot, demanding.

Delicious.

Her body, sizzling with a euphoric feeling that can only be described as *home*, molds against his. They fit into each other like puzzle pieces, forming the most beautiful image that she never wants to look away from.

Tristan.

His smell, like vanilla and sandalwood, fills her senses. His taste saturates her mouth as his tongue dances with hers, and she only knows that she wants more of it.

Her hands travel down his chest, pushing hungrily at the firmness under the cotton of his shirt, until they find the bottom of it, sneaking up under until they reach the skin they crave to touch.

A moan escapes his lips, echoing in her open mouth, and it's like her touch is a gunshot unleashing race hounds that were anxiously confined and now are set free.

He grips her hips and pushes her up against the nearest wall, toppling some framed maps. The crash doesn't register for either of them, they're so lost in each other. With heavenly abandon, she pulls his shirt off, taking a break from their feverish kissing to savor the sight of his bare chest. All the training he's spent his life on has sculpted him into a gorgeous masterpiece. His abs are so raised, looking like a freshly baked baguette, and she's tempted to take a nibble.

But he doesn't give her the chance. He devours her neck, sucking in a way that makes her eyelids flutter. She could melt into a puddle of the former Brielle and die happy. In fact, she just might.

This is perfect. This is heaven. This is everything she's ever wanted and more.

Tristan. Tristan. Tristan.

His name is a constant chant inside her head. But the words that come out, in the softest murmur, are, "I love you."

He stops, pulling away just enough to look into her eyes. His are lucid, molten, as they delve into hers, penetrating to her core, seeing all of her. And for a moment, she expects to hear him repeat the words.

But then, like curtains closing over a window, his eyes change, cooling from a boiling ocean to solid ice.

And just like that, the moment is over.

She feels suddenly very naked, even though he's the one without a shirt.

He hovers in front of her, awkward tension strung between them like a tightrope.

She feels the need to apologize, to say she didn't mean it, that it just came out, but they both know that would be a lie. She's never wished more that she could lie, and convincingly.

Doing the only thing she can do, she picks up his discarded shirt off the floor and hands it back to him.

He juggles the balled up cloth for a moment, watching it as it passes from hand to hand. "I should probably finish backing everything up," he says at last, his voice gravelly, his eyes avoiding hers.

She slips away from the wall, rubbing her arms that feel suddenly cold. "Right. I'm gonna go check on Jareth and Vee, see if they need help."

They both nod and go about their business as if the whole thing never happened.

27

LOGAN

Logan's breathing as if he ran the whole way from Ayers' house to FBI headquarters, when his car is actually parked right outside.

But it's not physical exertion that has him panting. It's the knowledge that he has proof.

His father was right. He's always been right.

Aliens exist. And they're roaming free through their city.

Logan presses the button for the lift several times, suddenly impatient. The sense of urgency is undeniable. Tristan and Brielle have to be arrested. They must be stopped.

The elevator emits a quiet ding and the doors slide open. For the first time since he left the woods, Logan hesitates. Cassandra was there. She's either an alien, too, or she's a sympathizer.

Although her link to Ayers was the whole reason he became involved with her, he didn't expect the sense of betrayal to be so strong. It's like a white-hot knife has punctured his chest.

Grimacing, he steps into the elevator. He was stupid to allow himself to get so emotionally involved with Cassandra. She was a target. A means to an end. Nothing more.

Logan scans his pass and the descent begins. He'll go straight to his father's office and tell him everything.

Like he should've done in the beginning.

As the elevator doors open, he tries to summon the excitement he felt just a few moments ago. His father is going to be so proud. Logan will be the one who gave him undeniable proof of his theories. Jack Cadbury will no longer be laughed at. He'll be recognized as the visionary he really is, the one who never stopped protecting Earth.

There's nothing greater Logan could ever give him.

Stepping into the corridor, Logan turns right. He'll go straight to his father's office. This conversation is a private one. One they'll both need to be sitting down for.

He swipes his hand over the sensor, and the flash of memory as his father had gifted him the chip that allows him to do this slices through his mind. His dad had blinked several times as he'd gently pushed the needle under the skin on the back of Logan's hand and inserted it. His father had swallowed, then blinked again.

"You're one of us now, son," he'd said, voice gruff with emotion.

Logan had been a little overwhelmed himself.

Which should only reinforce that he's doing the right thing.

He sucks in a sharp breath as the door opens, preparing himself, only to discover the office is empty. His cell dings, rupturing the unwelcome silence. It's his father.

Got an anonymous tip. Be back shortly.

Logan frowns. He didn't expect he'd have to wait. Glancing around the room, he wonders what's next. He can't go back out, Tristan saw his phone flash when he took the photo. They could be looking for him.

With his cell in his hand, Logan opens the image that's changed everything. It's a split-second photo that says it all. Tristan and Brielle have just touched ground and their suits have partially retracted. They're faces are exposed, their bodies still encased by alien technology.

Cassandra is beside them, smiling like the scene is perfectly normal. As if any of this is okay.

Logan's chest throbs like he's just been stabbed again as he thinks of other eyes seeing this scene. Very soon, others will know.

He realizes why the sense of betrayal is so strong, why it strikes so deep. He feels like he's betraying Cassandra. Wiping his hand down his face, Logan tells himself to get a grip.

They're possibly not even the same species!

Slapping his cell down on the desk, he starts to pace. Hopefully his dad will be here soon and can put him out of his misery. Once Logan's shared what he's seen, the agony will end. The knowledge he's done the right thing will alleviate all this pain. Nothing is going to stop him from going through with this.

No matter how long he has to wait.

Logan strides to the other side of the room, wondering if the corridor is a better place to work off these unwanted emotions. He spears his fingers through his hair, deciding that he doesn't want to answer any questions if someone sees him.

Reaching the two doors on the right of his father's office, he spins on his heel. And freezes as one of them clicks open.

Logan glances at the back of his hand. He must've inadvertently swiped past the sensor. Gripping the handle, he prepares to close it. His father hasn't shown him what's in here, which means he's not going to go snooping. Heck, it's probably the bathroom or a kitchenette.

But as Logan's eyes pass over the space that just opened, fully intending to close the door, he freezes for the second time.

And this time, he doesn't find the ability to move.

The room is all white—white walls, white tiled floor. And in the center sits an egg-shaped pod.

Logan's breath whooshes out. An alien pod.

Logan blinks. If his father has had this all along, no wonder he was so convinced aliens exist.

Inexplicably drawn to it, he finds himself circling the unbelievable sight. Smooth and pale, it glints in the fluorescent light. Sitting on a stand of some sort, it's about the size of an oval dining table. Even though it's as still as the walls around him, it feels like it's pulsing with energy.

Barely breathing, he reaches out to touch it. His fingers glide over the cool glass-like surface.

Silently but undeniably, it cracks open.

Logan jumps back, instantly regretting his action. He glances around frantically, wondering how he can undo what's already happening. But the pod continues to open, a portion of the top half sliding back.

From where he's standing, Logan catches a glimpse of the interior. More smooth ivory. A molded cradle of some sort. Panels lining the inside.

Logan knows he shouldn't be here, seeing this. He needs to call his dad, except his phone is still sitting on the desk. And for some reason, he's rooted to the spot.

And when he moves, it's not away from the pod. It's toward it. Inside he sees it's certainly what looks like a cradle, something that would curve around a baby. The compartments around it are ivory like the rest of the pod, all curved and smooth, all closed with no apparent way to open them. Only the one at the front is different. It has a symbol carved into it—a circle with a curve on top, resembling horns.

Knowing he shouldn't, and yet unable to stop himself, he traces the symbol. How can it be so foreign and yet so familiar, all at the same time?

It flares a dark burnished bronze and Logan yanks his hand back. What is he doing? Why can't he stop himself?

The compartment slides open, revealing what's inside.

It's a stone. No, a gem. A glorious, amber-colored jewel.

Logan thought he couldn't stop his movements before, but now it's like he's in a trance. As if his body is on autopilot. The pulsing gem beckons him like nothing has before.

He doesn't just brush his fingers over it, like he did the pod. He grasps it, picks it up, clasps it in his palm as if it's his. As if something that was taken from him has finally been returned.

The sensation is instantaneous and overwhelming. Warmth explodes like a tsunami bomb, rippling through every cell in Logan's body. Shades of bronze and copper and umber fill his vision as elation floods his mind. He gasps. He's never experienced anything so amazing and terrifying at the same time.

His back arches as the wave of power propels through him, his hand gripping the stone even tighter. He can barely breathe, and yet he's never felt more alive. It's like every inch of him was just bathed in truth.

The wave abates, leaving behind a strange tingling dancing up and down his skin. Logan looks down, expecting to find himself looking different. But his skin is unblemished, his clothes unaltered. He opens his palm, looking at the stone. "What just happened?" he whispers.

Before he can try to process an answer to the impossible question, something else moves in the pod. A compartment beside the first one slides open, a small lens appearing within.

Logan knows he should leave. Run. End what he should never have begun.

But still, he doesn't move.

Two people appear before him, a man and a woman, transparent in the way holographic images always are, but rich in color and detail. In fact, it's so sharp and precise that Logan sees the woman has the same color hair as he does, and it feels like he's looking into a mirror when his gaze falls on the man.

"No..." Logan breathes.

"Kadon, if you're watching this, then you're alive," the woman says with relief. "And you've reached Earth."

The man's arm tightens around the woman. "Please know we had no choice but to send you away. Chardis attacked the Gemini space station. Somehow, he knew the Zodiac heirs would be here for the christening."

They both duck as light flares behind them and the image flickers.

The woman clings to the man. "It was the only way to save you." Her face twists with pain. "The Zodiacs are our only hope."

The man ducks then pulls the woman in closer. "Son, do not let Chardis get his evil hands on the box. It is vital to your victory."

There's another, brighter flash, and the image shudders. "I know you've grown up to be a brave, wonderful man," the woman says, pride shining in her eyes. "Never stop fighting for what your heart knows is true." She presses her fingers to her lips and kisses the tips. She lifts them, her body fading away. "We love you."

And the image is gone.

Logan stumbles backward, his heart feeling like a runaway train trying to break free from his chest. Gripping the door, he closes it, the sound muffled against the roaring in his ears. Blindly, he stumbles to the lift. Inside the metal-lined space, he tries to get his breathing under control. His mind is in overdrive, and yet everything feels sluggish.

Something's happened. And no matter how right it felt, it's terribly wrong. His whole world has just collapsed. The foundations it was built on are gone. Destroyed. Actually, they never existed.

The elevators open and Logan lurches out, narrowly missing a woman who was about to enter.

The bustle of reality hits him like a slap as emotions flood him. Irritation as the frowning woman stalks to the back of the elevator. A flush of heated attraction as a couple make their way to the adjacent elevator. Tight anxiety as a young man rushes to the front doors.

Logan grips his head as he walks through the foyer. He's always sensed feelings. It's something he just put down to intuition. But now...now they're as sharp and clear as his own.

A mother with a young son exits the café to his left. They draw near as they head to leave the building, but the boy suddenly jerks to a stop. He looks around, confused and suddenly dazed. A moment later, he bursts into tears.

Bewildered himself, Logan steps around them as the woman kneels to comfort her son. Outside, he draws in great gulps of air. He pulls out his cell, ready to dial. There's only one person he can talk to right now.

He needs to talk to his sister.

But before he can press the familiar numbers, he hears his name. Although the word is only whispered, it ricochets through him.

He looks up, seeing Cassandra only a few feet away.
She looks hurt.
And she looks furious.

28

CASSANDRA

"Hey Logan, wanna 'hang'?" Cassandra sneers the last word, infusing it with as much poison as she can.

This viper has fangs.

His eyes are wide as he stands like a statue, staring at her. All color has drained from his face. No doubt he didn't expect to see her.

"C-Cassandra," he whispers.

She takes a step to her left, slowly circling her prey. "You know, I really thought we had something." She gives a dry, almost maniacal laugh. "You really got me." She claps her hands in mocking applause.

"Cassandra, whatever—" he begins to stammer.

"Save it!" she snaps. "I saw you in our security cams. I know you took a picture. And your sister outed you, by the way."

Impossibly, his face grows even paler.

"You were only dating me because your daddy asked you to," she sneers, crossing her arms in a way that she knows looks threatening, dangerous. "Were you a good little boy? Did you give daddy the dirt you found?"

He looks down, and a small part of her deep inside senses he's shocked beyond this encounter, but she's too furious to care about his petty problems.

"I was going to…" he says softly, but doesn't finish.

"Oh? You were going to?" she questions patronizingly, continuing her circling. "You expect me to believe that you didn't? That you grew a conscience and decided not to throw me under the bus? And let's not forget my friends, who have only ever worked hard to save you pieces of sh—"

"No, I didn't!" he yells, and she notices that his hands are trembling, that he twitches at every passerby across the street.

Curiosity invades her fury for a moment, and she truly looks at him, examining.

"I…I found something…" he says in a low voice, like he's ashamed.

She steps closer involuntarily, and it almost feels like the betrayal never happened. She feels the urge to comfort him. But she quickly stomps out that flame.

"What are you talking about?" She juts out a hip for good measure, showing she's not buying whatever act he's selling.

He regards her for a long silent moment, the sounds of the city amplifying as his chocolate eyes debate something internally.

Finally, he holds out a hand. "This."

In his palm sits a pretty, dark amber jewel. The glow of the bright street lights glint off of it, whispering its true majesty.

Cassandra is stunned into silence, unable to tear her eyes from it.

If they weren't in the busiest, most commercialized city in the world, a tumbleweed would have blown by in the long silence that follows.

"I'm guessing you know what this is," Logan says, his voice deep, accusing but hopeful at the same time.

Unable to speak, she nods twice, the arms she'd crossed for impact now hugging her. All the while, a voice in her head whispers, *It can't be, it can't be, it can't be...*

"Then maybe you could tell me?" His tone goes from demanding to pleading as he finishes the request.

She finally breaks her gaze away from the gem in his hand to look in his eyes. There, she finds a whole range of emotions she didn't see in her rage—fear, confusion, a need for answers.

Just like the way she felt when Brielle gave her the citrine.

"You're..." the words die in her tight throat.

He strides forward, closing the distance between them. "I'm what?" His chocolate eyes are desperate, pleading.

She swallows, trying to summon a courage that means betraying the wrath that's kept her going.

"Please?" he begs when she doesn't answer, wrapping his hands around hers and bringing them up, squeezing. "I know this is messed up. Trust me. But I *need* to know what this is."

"Where did you get this?" is all she can push through the dryness that cripples her tongue.

He nods, accepting that he'll have to be completely honest. "When I went in, no one was there, and...I accidentally opened some secret door in my dad's office..." His eyes dart back and forth as they look at her hands in his, searching for something she can't define, let alone see.

"What?" she implores, all traces of anger gone from her voice.

"There was this..." He swallows. "Pod." He grimaces, like the word tastes foul in his mouth. "And a recording."

Her eyes widen as much as they possibly can, her breath faltering on its passage to her suddenly deprived lungs.

"This man...he looked so much like—" He shakes his head

and squints, disbelieving. "They said all this stuff about Zodiacs and something called Chardis, and…"

She straightens her back. "How did you feel when you touched the gem?" She's almost afraid of the answer, and more afraid of what it will mean.

He throws his head back, and for a moment, all traces of fear are gone. "Amazing!" he almost hisses. "Like I found a part of me that I never knew was missing."

Their eyes meet, and that same electricity she'd felt before sizzles between them.

"What does this mean?" His voice is small, and he looks broken. It makes her want to put him back together.

She bites her lip, knowing this is a betrayal worse than the one he performed on her, but she's helpless to fight it. "It means you're a Zodiac Guardian."

He shakes his head, looking like she just slapped him. "No." He continues shaking his head. "No. I'm a future FBI agent. I'm a member of Nebula. I can't be one of you!"

Now she feels like she was slapped. "One of us?" she barks. "Oh right, you were about to roll over on us. On me!"

"I didn't want to!" His hands are balled into fists at his sides, but he looks more vulnerable than she's ever seen him. "Don't you get it? That's what's made this hard! I really like you."

She turtles in at the volume of his voice, instinctively bracing for the blows that usually follow such a sound.

But he doesn't raise a hand, or a belt, or anything.

He's not her father.

He's just a very confused boy, and one she hates herself for wanting to console, to placate.

"Then why?" she asks, her voice sounding more like a timid house kitten than a fierce lioness.

He looks down at his shoes, defeat molding his facial features. "My dad gave me everything. He took me in like his own son, sent me to college, recruited me into his secret organization without a second thought. I couldn't disappoint him."

"And now you're the one thing he's worked his whole life to destroy," she tacks on. But her tone isn't poisonous, isn't patronizing. She understands. As much as she hates this whole thing, she understands what he's going through. "I'm sorry."

He laughs dryly. "That's not the way this is supposed to work."

She shrugs. "That's what you get for dating me."

He rests his forehead against hers, and she doesn't balk.

"So, what? Does this mean I'm alien?" he asks solemnly.

"Unfortunately," she responds, her voice lilting into a question. Will he reject them? Reject her? Continue on his path to destroy everything they've worked toward building.

She waits for an impossibly long moment for the answer to these questions. In the distance, an ambulance siren wails, and she actually envies the poor soul it's about to retrieve, because she needs help more.

Finally, he pulls his forehead away from hers and looks into her anxious eyes.

"Tell me everything. I'm ready."

29

TRISTAN

I *love you.*

As Tristan watches the small bar reporting the download progress steadily grow, the three words echo in his head.

I love you.

Sweet pitch, his heart still levitates every time they flutter through him. He's never heard words that felt so true. So right. So perfect.

And yet, he didn't say them back. Couldn't. Even though they hovered on the tongue that was reveling in the taste of her.

His head drops into his hands with a groan. The Zodiacs have to leave the one place they all had roots—even him—and go on the run. And he has no idea where he and Brielle stand.

Every part of him sings when he's with her, and aches when they're apart. Anything feels possible when he's with Brielle. In fact, he's pretty sure galaxies are born every time they touch. If that's not love, what is? And yet those words are sacred. They should be saved for his soulmate.

Shouldn't they?

The progress bar stalls, like it has several times in the download process. The mountain of data that Alden accumulated is going to take a while to transfer. Which only gives Tristan more time to spend in no-freaking-idea land.

What he feels for Brielle is like nothing he's experienced before. An emotion so raw and right he can't get enough of it. But it can't be love, no matter how much he wants it to be. So that leaves him with one question.

Does he say it back?

There's the clatter of feet down the stairs, and Tristan spins around, bracing himself to see Brielle again. A part of him is already excited.

A part of him is thinking of making a run for the tunnel.

But it's not Brielle who appears in the doorway. Cassandra steps through, looking drained and tense. Tristan's about to ask her if anything is wrong when he sees who's behind her.

He shoots to his feet. Something is definitely wrong.

"You brought him here?" Tristan half-shouts, pointing at Logan. "What the pitch, Cassandra?"

Tristan expects Cassandra's usual fieriness to flare, but she simply shakes her head. "There's something you need to see."

Suddenly, there's more clattering down the stairs. Veronica, Jareth, and Brielle rush in.

"Is everything okay?" Brielle asks in a panic.

"Not so much," Tristan says as the three of them register who's already here.

"Logan?" Veronica asks, clearly confused. Her eyes widen, as if she just realized he's standing in the Zodiac's HQ. "You can't tell Dad about any of this. Please!"

Tristan is balancing on the balls of his feet as he tries to figure out why the pitch Cassandra has brought a spy into their lair. It's either too late, and Jack and soon the world will know about their true identities.

Or, he hasn't blabbed yet and they've just scored themselves a prisoner.

In either scenario, Tristan is going to develop a headache.

Logan shakes his head, glancing at each Zodiac in turn. "I haven't spoken to Dad. And I'm not going to."

"Why not?" Tristan shoots back at him.

Logan glances at Cassandra and she nods. Tristan notes the current that passes between them, and he doesn't like it. If Cassandra has feelings for this guy, then it's going to cloud her judgment. The Leo in their pack doesn't do things by halves.

Logan draws in a deep breath and extends his hand. "Because of this."

He opens his palm, revealing a walnut-sized amber jewel.

Shock spears through Tristan, hotly followed by anger. "Where did you get that?"

"That's why I'm here. I was looking for my dad in his Nebula office when I found a room. It had a pod in it. And inside the pod was a recording, and this."

Instinctively, Tristan turns to Brielle. She looks at him, green eyes wide and disbelieving.

"He's telling the truth."

Cassandra steps a little closer to Logan. "Yes, he is."

But for some reason, Tristan is having a hard time getting his head around this. The Taurus just walked into HQ? And the Taurus is Jack Cadbury's son? What the hell is Nebula? And holy pitch, Jack has a pod?

"Say the word 'Akash,'" Tristan orders.

Logan looks at him quizzically, but complies. "Akash."

He leaps back as his loud gasp is swallowed by his suit. "What the—"

The metamorphosis is over in a blink. Logan looks down.

He runs his hands over his arms, his chest. He glances behind as if to make sure the front is the same as the back. He sees what the other Zodiacs do. He's now totally encased in bronze.

"Was that really necessary?" Cassandra arches a brow at Tristan.

Tristan shrugs. "It's the best way to make sure."

She turns back to Logan. "If you say it again, the suit retracts."

Logan does so, and it reveals his stunned face. Veronica rushes to him. "Holy crap, you're one of them!" She pauses. "But, Mom…"

"Seems she's not my biological mother," Logan croaks. "She never told me."

"This is a bit of a mind meld, big bro."

Logan nods, swallowing. "It's a lot to get my head around."

Veronica grins. "Although, it's also kinda cool. What's your superpower?"

"Superpower?"

"I see visions of the future." Tristan says. And it sure would've been nice to have had some inkling this bombshell was coming. "Brielle senses lies."

Tristan glances at Jareth, who with a wave of his hand, creates a Rubik's cube. As they all watch in silent fascination, he quickly solves it as it floats midair. Even Tristan is impressed.

Next, he turns to Cassandra. "Cassandra's power isn't one we want to demonstrate within such confined space," he says wryly. "Let's just say it's our most offensive weapon so far. Oh, and you may want to invest in a good set of sunglasses."

Veronica jiggles on her toes. "So, what about you?"

Logan frowns, glancing down at the stone. "I'm not really sure."

Tristan represses a sigh. A new Zodiac who doesn't know what his powers are is just what he needs.

Logan straightens. "Hang on a sec." His gaze falls on Veronica. "You're excited at the news."

She rolls her eyes. "You just joined Team Vee. Of course I am." Her brows contract infinitesimally. "I'm sure we can figure something out with Dad."

Logan's gaze moves to Jareth. "You're apprehensive."

Jareth's body twitches in surprise, but Tristan waits. Logan is doing what any phony clairvoyant would do—make good assumptions. Just like Tristan, Jareth is well aware of what this means. Logan's still Jack's son. And until a couple of hours ago, he was determined to find the Zodiacs purely so he could help destroy them.

Logan looks at Brielle and his brows contract. "You're...sad."

Tristan's gut clenches, but before he can say anything, Logan's moved onto Cassandra. "You're..." his face softens. "Hopeful."

Tristan suspects that has more to do with her heart than the Zodiacs.

Logan's dark gaze falls on Tristan. "And you're suspicious. Defensive. There's a thread of hope. But you're also nervous and uneasy. And..." He angles his head, studying him closely.

Tristan crosses his arms. He's everything Logan just listed, but the concerns are what are forefront in his mind. They can't let a spy into their team, Zodiac or not. Too much is at stake.

Logan narrows his eyes, his gaze turning intense. Tristan simply glares back. If he wants to play a staring game, then bring it on.

But as he stands there, a tingling trips up his toes. It shoots up his legs, growing as it finds more room to expand in his torso. There, it explodes, sending frantic fireworks zipping through every part of him. His heart rate increases as energy charges through his muscles. When it reaches Tristan's face, it draws up a huge, involuntary smile.

Before he knows what's happening, he's launched forward and grabbed Logan's hand, pumping it enthusiastically. "I'm so excited you're here!" he gushes. "I can't believe we have the fifth Zodiac with us!" Tristan glances around at the others, registering their shocked faces but not caring. "Zarius and Tess would be overjoyed!"

Logan releases his hand, and the excitement drains as quickly as it had rushed through Tristan. He blinks, trying to figure out what just happened.

Logan's mouth curves. "It seems I can manipulate emotions."

If Tristan wasn't so gob smacked—on top of trying to figure out what this will mean for their team—he'd have time to be embarrassed at that cheerleader-level exuberance. He's kind of glad he doesn't. He just connected with an inner Labrador he never knew he had.

Logan's gaze circles the room. "The recording I mentioned," he says somberly. "It had a message." He looks at Tristan. "From my birth parents."

The Zodiacs all glance at each other. Logan has seen his real parents, something none of them have experienced.

Then there's the pod itself.

And something called Nebula.

Tristan nods. "Tell me everything."

JACK

18:03

· · ·

Jack scans the hulking warehouse, recognizing it for what it is. A place where prying eyes wouldn't dare go. A place so full of angles and shadows, it's easy to hide.

The perfect place for an anonymous tip.

I have information on the Zodiacs.

He walks away from his car, eyes scanning every dark corner. He could use a lead on the Zodiacs, but he has no intention of going inside that building to get it.

He stands in the center of the empty parking lot. "I'm here."

Silence.

Jack's hand hovers close to his gun, ears pricked. There's a soft crunch of gravel and he spins around, gun pointed. "Show yourself!"

"With pleasure," comes a bodiless voice.

A second later, a man materializes. Jack doesn't have time to process the shock because pain splinters through his skull. He drops to his knees, the blow to the back of his head seeming to temporarily paralyze as agony ricochets through him. There's a clatter as his gun falls to the ground.

"Bring him in," says a voice that's vaguely familiar.

Jack can only watch as another fist flies toward his jaw. He crumples onto the black asphalt, conscious and yet helpless as one of the men grabs him by the back of his jacket and drags him along.

Jack's vision swims, shadows shifting and blurring as he tries to regain control of his body. He can feel his legs scraping across the gravel, knows his arms are hanging limply by his side, but it's like they're disconnected. He's little more than a boneless liability.

He's vaguely aware that he's being pulled through a door and then his feet are thumping down stairs. He's being taken into the warehouse.

A place where no one knows he is. Where no one will find his dead body for months.

He's hauled up and slammed into a chair. There's the sound of tape tearing off a roll and his arms are strapped down. Next are his legs. His mind screams for him to fight. Once he's strapped down, escape will be almost impossible.

His fingers twitch and his legs jerk, but that's all. Within minutes, he's trussed and completely immobile.

A sharp slap across his face returns the consciousness he was grasping at so desperately. Jack lifts his head, blinking as he brings the world into focus.

A man shoves his face close to his. "Get yourself together, Cadbury," he snarls. "We have some talking to do."

The realization of who's captured him is like a dousing of ice water. "Solomon."

"I'd offer you a drink," he drawls. "But this establishment doesn't seem to have a bar."

Jack yanks the bonds holding him, but the tape has been wrapped tightly. All he can do is grip the arms of the chair with fury and frustration. "You're a lawyer. You know what it means to take a federal officer hostage."

Solomon laughs. "I am not answerable to your laws."

"No one is above the law," Jack grinds out.

"Those who work for a higher power are," Solomon croons. "Chardis is the law."

Chardis.

"Who is this Chardis?" Jack demands. "And what does he want with me?"

Solomon steps back, looking thoughtful. Jack takes the opportunity to do a surreptitious scan. Several men are scattered around the warehouse floor, with who knows how many more in the shadows or outside.

Jack blinks. And one seemed to materialize out of thin air when he was attacked.

"You will soon know who Chardis is," Solomon promises. "The whole universe will. Until then, my orders were to find the Zodiacs." He angles his head, studying Jack. "Although then I was tasked with a new target. Nebula."

Jack meets his gaze. "I don't know what you're talking about."

"In fact, Clara worked for me. She found the pod." Solomon's lip curls. "And then you killed her."

Jack doesn't respond. He needs his wits about him, right now. This situation is far more dangerous than he anticipated.

These people aren't human.

Solomon rubs his chin, studying Jack like he's a specimen. "Then you brought Brielle in for questioning, and I knew we couldn't have her near the pod. Not until I was ready."

"I don't know what you're talk—"

Solomon moves so swiftly, Jack doesn't even know he has until a fist connects with his cheek. His head snaps to the side, pain surging through him and yanking out an involuntary groan.

"Let's skip the false ignorance, shall we?" Solomon grips Jack's face. "I want the pod," he drawls. "More specifically, I want what's in the pod."

Jack's face throbs. His head feels like it was struck with far more than a fist. But he ignores all of it. He speaks slowly, enunciating each word. "I don't know what you're talking about."

Solomon's hand tightens, his fingers digging into Jack's cheeks. Fury flashes in his cold eyes. But he doesn't hit him, which tells Jack what he suspected.

They need him alive.

"I need the pod and I need the Zodiacs to open it. That's why you're here."

"As bait?" Jack scoffs. "The Zodiacs won't care about me. They'd love to have me off their backs."

Solomon releases Jack's jaw and steps back. He adjusts his cuffs, a calculating smile spreading across his face. "You're probably right."

Jack's body remains coiled. He's not fooled by Solomon's mild tone. The bastard already has a plan B.

He pulls out his cell, stretching his neck from side to side as he dials a number. "But Logan will most certainly come running."

30

LOGAN

As he finishes, Logan scans each stunned face. Their emotions form a thick jumble, making the air heavy and weighing it down.

They're shocked.

Astonished.

Bewildered in a way that makes Logan's head spin.

If his ability to sense emotions hadn't become so much stronger, he would've assumed these feelings were his own, in part because he's experiencing every one of those. In a short space of time, not only has he told them everything he saw in the room beside his father's office, he's also learned words he didn't know existed.

Skins.

Chardis.

He now knows the fate of the Universe depends on the Zodiacs.

What's more, he's one of them.

And yet, to join them means turning his back on the only man he's called his father.

"So, what now?" Brielle asks quietly.

Logan can't help but marvel at how steady her voice is. This girl is holding so much grief he assumes she must've recently lost someone very dear to her. Instinctively, he extends a soothing warmth to her, seeing her shoulders relax a little as her emotional turmoil dials down.

An echoing pain flares in Tristan before he quickly quashes it. "Well, it doesn't look like we're going on the run, so that's something," he muses. "And I suppose we need to train our latest addition." He sizes Logan up. "Can you fight?"

"I've been through the defensive and offensive techniques course at the college," Logan says mildly. He's also done training in his own time—desperate to make his dad proud—but his own pain flares at the thought so he doesn't mention it. Tristan will find out what he's capable of when they undertake their first session.

Tristan narrows his eyes. "And we have to decide what we're going to do about Jack."

Logan's stomach constricts. That's a question he doesn't have an answer to.

His cell vibrates in his pocket but he ignores it. He has four Zodiacs and his sister looking at him expectantly.

Veronica shakes her head. "Dad can't know."

And yet Logan is a Nebula operative. His cell vibrates again, but Logan doesn't look away from his sister's pleading gaze. "I'd be a spy."

Against their own father.

"I'll admit, it's not easy. But we're talking about the fate of the Universe, here." She shrugs. "And maybe one day, Dad will be able to see the truth—the Zodiacs aren't the bad guys."

When Logan's phone rings for the third time, he frowns. He pulls it out of his pocket, glancing at the others apologetically. "Sorry. Someone is really trying to get a hold of me."

He sees his father's name on the screen, and his gut

tightens even more. He'd only ring repeatedly if it were an emergency.

Logan takes the call. "Dad?"

Alarm flashes across Veronica's face just as Tristan steps forward, a warning flashing across his face.

"Jack can't talk right now," says a voice Logan's never heard. "He's all tied up." The man chuckles coldly. "Quite literally."

Ice shoots through Logan's veins. "Who is this? And what have you done to my father?"

Veronica's hand claps over her mouth, the white of her eyes expanding above.

"Jack's fine...for now," the man purrs. "But he's only going to stay, well, intact, if I get what I want."

Veronica waves her hand frantically, indicating for Logan to put the call on speakerphone. He glances at Tristan, who gazes back at him steadily. The cold, hard determination Logan senses actually settles his thundering pulse a little.

Logan presses the button. "What do you want?"

"The pod, of course."

The man's voice carries through the room and Veronica's eyes widen once more. She looks to Brielle and they mouth a name to each other.

Logan frowns. "I don't know what you're talking about."

"Jack tried that line, too," the man growls, his voice turning cold. "You have four hours to bring it to me or you'll be finding pieces of your father for weeks to come. I'll text you the address."

The line goes dead and Logan is left staring at his cell as the screen goes dark.

Veronica tucks herself into Jareth's side as he wraps his arms around her. "Dad," she whispers. She shakes her head, her voice regaining some strength. "I knew that Solomon was a slimeball."

Tristan glances at Brielle. "The lawyer who got you out?"

She nods. "Yes, that was most definitely him."

"But if he's working for Chardis, then why would he let you go?"

Logan's hand is wrapped so tightly around his cell the vibration of the text feels like it rattles his very marrow. He opens the message from his father. The one Solomon just sent.

"It's an address in the industrial area. Probably an abandoned warehouse." He looks at the others, then at Cassandra. "I'm sorry. I have to give this Solomon guy what he wants. I don't have a choice."

Logan braces himself, knowing he's just chosen Jack over the Zodiacs. Dammit, over Cassandra.

"We'll help you," Tristan says and the others nod. Cassandra's hands even clench as she silently conveys her commitment.

"You will?" That wasn't what Logan was expecting to hear.

"Look, Jack Cadbury isn't on my people-I-want-to-hug-this-century list. But Solomon has him because of the Zodiacs." Tristan's mouth settles in a firm line. "Plus, you're one of us now. Your fight is our fight."

Logan blinks, trying to assimilate that.

"And I'm guessing the pod is at Nebula HQ."

"Yes, it is."

Tristan grins. "A part of me likes knowing I'll have been in there without Jack knowing."

"Tristan," Veronica hisses. "You need to give Logan time to come to terms with this before you make those jokes."

Except Logan doesn't have the luxury of time. They have four hours to get the pod out of Nebula and to the warehouse.

"Sorry," Tristan says, looking only mildly apologetic. His

face turns serious. "This is going to be tricky. We can't deploy our suits, not unless it's life or death." He glances at Cassandra then Jareth. "Nor can we use our powers in front of Jack. That way, he can't pin anything on us."

Everyone falls silent as they digest this.

Jareth frowns. "Let's hope there aren't too many Skins, then."

The humans who have been corrupted by dark matter. The ones with super strength and speed, and who can turn invisible. This is sounding more and more dangerous.

Brielle pulls back her shoulders. "We've got this."

Logan's surprised to find a thread of hope, maybe even conviction, lighting up the dark anguish that sits heavily in her. Brielle means what she says, despite what they're facing...and what she carries.

"Brielle's right," Tristan says, his voice strengthening. "Let's go kick Solomon's ass and get that pod while we're there."

The others file up the stairs, silent but determined. Logan hangs back, glad to see Cassandra does the same.

All the barriers that kept them apart no longer exist. And yet...

"Cassandra," he starts, only to find the words quickly dry up. "I'm sorry for all the lies." He extends his hands, palms up. "I had no idea."

She nods, her lion-colored eyes guarded. "Neither of us did."

Logan takes a step forward, and his heart clenches as Cassandra quickly retreats. His hands drop.

She swallows. The turmoil he senses is twisting and churning so fast he can't untangle the emotions. "We're strictly teammates, Logan, nothing more. I don't know if I can trust you. Not yet."

Logan nods in understanding. An ache permeates his

chest, digging its claws into his ribs like it doesn't plan on leaving any time soon.

Sadness flashes through Cassandra as she rushes past him and flies up the stairs.

Logan remains where he is, mute and frozen. He should've called her back. He should've told her he'd fight for her, for what they've found together.

But the truth is, he's not sure he can trust himself.

His father is a hostage with his life on the line. The Zodiacs may have to fight to free him.

And yet if Logan chooses one, he'll betray the other.

31

CASSANDRA

I t's quite a feat to get them all through the FBI lobby. Jareth has to use immense focus to make each of their faces look like completely different people. All except for Logan, who's their ticket in.

Brielle walks nervously in front of Cassandra, looking like a limping gazelle crossing a den of hungry lions. Cassandra can't blame her for being anxious. They're all walking right into the hands of the organization that wants to lock them up and throw away the key. And if Jareth loses focus for even a second, they'll be exposed. Trapped. Surrounded by FBI agents with guns.

Mercifully, the elevator doors slide open, and they eagerly step inside.

Just before the doors close, a hand pushes between them, stopping them. The doors lazily open once more, and a heavy set man who reeks of stale coffee flashes Logan a look of recognition before entering.

"Well, if it isn't young Cadbury," he says, stuffing his hands in his front pockets. Cassandra doesn't like the smug tone he's aiming at Logan. And by the look on Logan's face, he doesn't either.

"Flanagan," Logan acknowledges begrudgingly.

"Where'd your old man run off to? Out chasing more aliens?" He laughs heartily and slaps Logan's shoulder like they're old pals.

Logan's eyes narrow and he shuffles away from the pudgy, asinine agent. "He's doing his job. Shouldn't you be doing the same?"

Agent Flanagan's laughter dies, and he turns his puffy-cheeked face in Logan's direction. "I'd tread lightly, if I were you, boy," he warns. "You're only an intern. And if you think being Cadbury's son gives you any kind of special treatment, you couldn't be more wrong."

The air inside the suddenly very cramped elevator becomes tense, and everyone but Cassandra and Veronica pretend not to have heard the slight.

Despite the fact that Logan lied to her and used her, and only didn't expose her because he found out he's just as guilty as she is, Cassandra can't help but feel the urge to kick this guy in the crotch for ridiculing him.

But she reigns in her anger. The last thing they need right now is an altercation with an agent. The best thing would be to ignore the guy until he gets to his floor and waddles out of their way, which Logan is impressively taking the lead in.

The elevator stops and the doors open.

"Smell ya later, Cadbury," Agent Flanagan dismisses as he disembarks.

The doors close, and no one really takes a breath until the elevator starts to descend again.

"Jerk," Veronica grumbles behind clenched teeth.

The silence that follows is awkward. No one wants to mention the elephant in the cramped elevator.

Cassandra had no idea that the rest of the FBI thought

Logan's dad was an alien conspiracy lunatic. He'd sent the FBI after Tristan and Jareth. She assumed that meant he had some pull, some authority, or at the least, was respected.

"I'm sorry," she whispers to Logan.

All he does is sigh, but somehow that puff of breath says everything he's feeling. That he's worried about his dad, first and foremost. That he hates the way the other agents talk about him and wants to change it. And that he knows he's giving up his only chance to do that by siding with them.

"So, once we get to the pod, how are we going to get it out of Nebula?" Tristan asks, and everyone in the elevator relaxes, grateful for a subject change. "I doubt Nebula will let us just cart the thing out."

"There was no one here earlier, when I discovered it," Logan says. "And at this hour, I doubt there will be now. But if anyone is around, I'll just distract them while the rest of you get it to the elevator."

"Okay, so we get it to the elevator," Jareth says, his disguise fading. "Then what? We can't exactly cart a giant alien space pod through the FBI main lobby."

"Yeah, that'll go over real well," Veronica adds.

"We're not going through the lobby," Logan replies. "We'll go through the parking garage. If we take the stairwell, that'll make it less likely for us to run into anyone. Then we'll borrow one of the stake out vans."

"Sounds like a plan," Tristan says with a satisfied nod.

When the elevator stops, the floor is indeed empty. But that doesn't stop them all from running down the hall as fast as they can. Not only is there the fear that someone might walk in on them at any moment, but there's also a ticking time bomb on Logan and Veronica's dad's life. They don't have any time to waste.

In one of the offices, Logan opens a hidden door, and beyond it in a small room sits a giant white egg. They all enter the secret compartment and file in around the pod, and for a moment, they forget their haste.

Cassandra has never seen a space pod before. Or at least, not since she was too young and small to remember. She's guessing most of the others haven't either.

So this is what they all came to Earth in. Incredible! She can't help but wonder if this one is still operational. If it could take her back. She could be with her real family... If they're even still alive...

"Guys, this is cool and all," Veronica's voice slices the silence. "But the clock's ticking. Let's get the heck outta here."

"Right," Tristan says.

They all close in against the pod and pick it up. Logan guides them out of the small room, then down the hall and into the elevator. The only way they all fit now is if half of them squeeze into the corners and the other half climb on top of the pod.

The ascent is a painstakingly slow one, and Cassandra swears everyone can hear her heart pounding as they get closer and closer to the second floor. If they run into anyone, they're toast. No way is someone going to just look away from a frickin' space pod. There will be questions asked, and ultimately they'll lose everything.

Cassandra is prepared to blast someone if she has to. But she really hopes she isn't forced to make that choice.

When the elevator stops at the second floor, they all hold their breath as the doors slowly part.

"Oh, thank pitch," Brielle exhales.

"Pitch?" Logan asks.

"Yeah, it's kinda their thing. I'll explain later," Veronica says. "Now come on."

They hop off the pod and hoist it up again, carrying it as quickly as they can to the stairwell. Luckily, they make it without running into a single soul.

Logan opens the stairwell door and they collectively try to squeeze it through.

"Oh no," Cassandra hears Brielle fret, followed by a growl from Tristan.

"It won't fit," Veronica grouses.

Cassandra sees the dismay wrinkling Logan's handsome features, and she hates that she still feels compelled to do whatever it takes to console him.

She takes a step back to analyze the situation. The pod is just barely too big to fit through the door frame. It needs only a couple more inches of clearance on each side.

"What's plan B?" Tristan calls over the pod to Logan on the other side.

"Move the pod away from the door, guys," Cassandra instructs.

"Why?" Logan asks.

"I'm plan B."

The others knowingly carry the pod quite a distance away from the doorframe, and Cassandra moves in, very aware of Logan's curious gaze locked on her.

"Bro, you might want to step back," Veronica cautions her brother, who's still standing a foot away inside the stairwell.

His eyes narrowing even further, he does as he's told.

Positioned in the middle of the doorway, Cassandra places her hands on opposite sides of the frame where the pod had scuffed the paint. She doesn't think about the fact that she's about to use her powers in front of the guy she most recently made out with, doesn't worry about what this reveal will make him think of her. She has a job to do, and that's all she focuses on as she wills her hands to heat up.

They begin to glow like a red hot iron, and the paint and wood and plaster sizzle and melt away under her touch. Wider and wider the frame gives in, creating gaps just big enough for the pod to fit through. Cassandra withdraws her hands and lets them cool.

Then she steps back. She sheepishly looks up at Logan, and his chocolate eyes are wide. Before her cheeks can turn as red as her hands just were, she turns away. "Okay, try it now."

Her friends heave the pod back toward the frame, and this time, it slips through with some careful maneuvering.

The trek down the stairs is no less harrowing. They clumsily carry the pod down, tripping over steps or each other's feet, smashing hands against the wall or the railing. But eventually they make it to the entrance to the parking garage.

Logan peeks out to make sure there's no one around, then Cassandra repeats her doorframe melting trick and they carry the pod across the pavement to an empty van. Logan opens the back doors, and after several forceful shoves, they get the pod inside. The doors just barely close.

They all pant in relief, Brielle leaning against the side of the van and Veronica doubled over with her hands on her knees. They don't have the cardio that the rest of them do.

"Alright, let's go," Logan prompts, opening the driver's door and climbing in.

Cassandra is both relieved and disappointed when Tristan takes the front passenger seat. She has no idea what Logan thinks of her now that he's seen what she can do. He hated aliens because he thought they were dangerous. Well, in her case, he was right. Would he hate her now? Fear her? She hates that she even cares.

The rest of them pile into the van wherever they fit, and Logan drives toward the exit.

Once they get onto the open road, everyone breathes a little bit easier. They actually stole something priceless from an FBI building. Who else can say that?

But as harrowing as that was, Cassandra knows it was nothing compared to the challenge they're about to face next.

"You can't seriously send him in there all alone!"

Cassandra is beside herself as they sit down the road from the warehouse. Her stomach is in knots, but her rage boils the bile to vapors before it can come up.

"We have to," Tristan insists, fastening a spy cam to Logan's lapel. "If we all go in, we'll completely lose the element of surprise."

"But he's a brand new Zodiac," Cassandra argues, practically yelling, her voice echoing down the empty road.

"Shh!" they all hiss at her.

She lowers her voice, but not her inflection, and continues. "He has no idea how to use his powers, or how to fight Skins. They'll destroy him!"

"Well, I have some idea—" Logan interjects.

"He's going in to negotiate for his father," Tristan reasons. "If the Skins see us with him, the whole thing will immediately turn into a fight, and they might just kill Jack right then and there."

Both Logan's and Veronica's faces pale at that.

"Well, then I'll go with him," Cassandra counters.

Tristan shakes his head. "The Skins know who we all are. If they see even one of us, they'll know all of us are involved, and Logan's cover will be blown. Right now, they don't know that he knows who he is. We need to take advantage of that."

Cassandra ruffles, ready to contest, but Logan puts his hand on her shoulder, and she instantly calms. She can't be sure if it's his power at work, or the natural reaction of the chemistry they share.

"Cassandra, this isn't my first rodeo," he says coolly. "I've been in negotiations before. Admittedly with less dangerous criminals. But I know how to handle myself, and how to talk. I'll be alright."

"Plus, the instant things turn, we'll barge in and do our superhero thing," Jareth adds.

Cassandra huffs and pouts, but doesn't argue any further. She knows that this is the only way. "Fine."

Tristan steps back from Logan and examines him. "Okay, I can hardly see it. I think you're good."

Logan nods, and Cassandra is impressed at how confident he looks despite the fact he's about to try to save his dad from aliens.

Veronica approaches him and throws her arms around him. "Be careful, bro. And get our dad back safe and sound."

"I will," he promises. He withdraws and gets into the driver's side of the van, then drives down the road to the warehouse.

They watch as the bay doors open to invite him, then swallow him whole like some mythical monster.

Cassandra snatches the laptop from Brielle and plops onto the curb, eyes glued to the spy cam feed. The rest of them crowd around her to watch as well.

A squad of Skins stand inside the open, brightly lit space, with Solomon at the forefront, and Jack bound and gagged to a chair at the back. Logan gets out of the van as Solomon swaggers closer.

"There had better be a pod in that van," Solomon warns, so close to Logan that the feed only shows him from the neck down. "Cause if this is some kinda Trojan Horse situation, dear old daddy is already dead." How the hell can this guy still sound charming even as he's making a threat? Damn southern drawl!

Logan steps aside, and Cassandra can imagine him raising his hands in surrender. "Take a look for yourself."

Solomon looks to his goons and gives them a nod, and a handful of them swarm the van as they head to the back. They open the doors and Logan follows Solomon as he rounds to the back, then smiles when he sees the pod. "You did good, son."

"Now, I want my father back," Logan demands, voice unwavering.

Solomon puts up his hands in a slow-down gesture. "Not so fast, son. We need you to open it."

"The deal was the pod for my dad," Logan says. "You can open it when we're gone."

Solomon shakes his head, making a tutting sound. "No, in fact the deal was for a particular item inside the pod. We need to make sure you didn't take it out."

Cassandra swallows hard. They must want his stone. They'll see he took it and know that he knows. She shifts her position, ready to jump in and save him.

The Skins carry out the pod and set it in the center of the room. Solomon gestures for Logan to open it. Logan walks up and touches the pod, gently caressing it, and the top smoothly rises to reveal the cradle.

Solomon reaches in, feeling around the seemingly seamless interior. He looks like he knows exactly what he's searching for.

This is it. Cassandra holds her breath.

A compartment pops open under Solomon's touch. But it's not empty. Inside sits a beautifully ornate box made of some type of metal. If Cassandra didn't know, she'd think it was a very expensive jewelry box.

"What in the pitch is that?" Tristan whispers, voicing the question they're all thinking.

Solomon removes the box, holding it up and beaming like he's just found some ancient treasure. He probably has.

"Thank you, son," Solomon praises. "Chardis will be very pleased."

He tries to open it, but the thing is sealed tight. From this angle, Cassandra can't tell if it takes a key or not.

After struggling for a few seconds to no avail, he offers the box to Logan. "Open it."

Logan hesitantly accepts the box and attempts the same. No matter what approach he takes or how much force he employs, the box refuses to open.

"I said open it," Solomon demands.

"I can't," Logan grunts as he tries once more.

Solomon yanks the box back. "So be it."

Logan doesn't waste any time. "Release my dad now."

"Of course." Solomon snaps his fingers, and the goons close in on Logan.

Cassandra doesn't wait to hear what's said next. She jumps to her feet and sprints for the warehouse. The other Zodiacs are fast behind her. She blasts a fireball at the bay door, creating a hole large enough for them all to storm in.

As soon as they enter, the ceiling windows shatter, raining down glass on everyone's heads. When Cassandra looks up, she sees men in black bulletproof uniforms are zipping down ropes from the busted windows, equipped with large guns.

More Skins? FBI? It doesn't matter.

All she cares about is saving Logan.

32

LOGAN

L ogan ducks his head as glass rains down on him, but he
doesn't slow. He needs to get to his father. He feels one
or two shards of pain as the fragments pepper his shoulders,
the remainder shattering on the cement floor in a shower of
crystals. The Nebula operatives land a second later, cutting
the black ropes they abseiled down. They're instantly
moving, heading toward Jack, their leader.

A quick glance over Logan's shoulder shows the Zodiacs
streaming through the hole that was just blasted through the
wall.

He has no idea where Solomon is.

Logan keeps his gaze on his father, as if his unbroken
focus will get him there faster. A man materializes next to
Jack. A Skin. For a second Logan considers shouting, but
there's no point. His father is still strapped to the chair.

He's a sitting duck.

The Skin steps behind Logan's father and takes hold of
his head, bringing a knife to his throat.

This time the denial is involuntary. "No!"

His father struggles in the chair, only to quickly stop as

the blade on his neck is pushed in tighter. He holds himself still, his head held firmly against the Skin's chest. His eyes are wide with the knowledge that no one can get to him in time.

Logan focuses on the Skin, desperately trying to see if there's any emotion he can work with. At first, he feels nothing. As if the man is hollow.

The dark matter possessing him has made him a soulless cavern.

But then Logan detects the flicker of something. The faintest quiver of...disgust. There's a part of the Skin that is sickened by what he's about to do.

Still running, Logan injects everything he has into the blast of energy he sends toward the Skin. The man jolts as if something just detonated inside of him. He shakes his head, as if trying to rid himself of the sensation.

Except Logan amplifies it, and the feeling of disgust becomes so powerful it almost makes him nauseous himself.

The Skin releases his father and stumbles back. He leans over, hands on his knees, his whole body heaving as he vomits.

Logan reaches his father a handful of seconds later—seconds that would've been enough time to end Jack Cadbury's life. Knocking out the still heaving Skin, he snatches the knife and makes short work of the tape holding his father's arms.

Around him are the sounds of battle—grunts, fists connecting with flesh, cries as someone is hurt—but apart from quick glances to ensure there's no immediate threat, Logan focuses on freeing his father. In fact, he quickly realizes they've been surrounded by Nebula agents. A circle of protection so Logan can complete his task.

He carefully slices the tape around his father's face. The moment it's cut, his father tears it away, barely grimacing at the pain.

"You brought Ayers and the others?" he demands. "What were you thinking?"

Logan cuts away the tape strapping his father's legs to the chair. "That I might need some help saving your life," he shoots back.

His father stands, rubbing his wrists. "We have everything under control," he says, indicating the ring of agents around them.

Logan spins around, placing his back against his father's. Now isn't the time to argue about this. He did what he thought was right to save him.

Logan glances at the Zodiacs. They're caught up in a battle of their own near the hole they entered.

"Run!" Tristan shouts. "Get out of here!"

Maybe if Jack wasn't around, they could deploy their suits and even out this fight a little more.

"I'm not owing Ayers any favors," Logan's father mutters behind him. "Once we finish with these guys, that kid is going down."

There's no chance for Logan to respond, because more Skins materialize. Their numbers seem to double in a blink, like some deadly optical illusion.

Except, the fury they're surrounded by is very real. It throbs with heat, making Logan's own anger flare. He flexes his shoulders, tamping it down. He needs to keep his wits about him if they're going to get out of this alive.

He and his father steadily spin around, fists raised. Everywhere, Skins and Nebula agents are fighting.

Except Nebula is outnumbered.

And outpowered.

A Skin picks one up by the throat and throws him across the room. The agent's body crumples as it slams into the concrete floor, sliding a few feet before coming to a halt. His body remains still and lifeless.

Another agent to Logan's left points his gun at the nearest Skin. The Skin disappears, reappearing a second later right in front of him. The agent fires but the Skin is already knocking the man's arm upward. Logan ducks as the gun goes off. One strike from the Skin to the agent's throat and the man is on the ground, writhing and choking.

More gunshots ricochet as the Nebula agents resort to gunfire. Logan and his father duck instinctively, knowing they're in a vulnerable position, but having nowhere to run.

Flashes of fear start to stab through the Skin's fury and Logan realizes it's his fellow agents. They're losing.

There's a cry to his right, then two more to his left. The men and women he'd barely gotten to know, those who swore to protect Earth from the very evil they're surrounded by, are dropping one by one.

Bodies accumulate around them, some bloodied and groaning, most unmoving and lifeless.

Logan presses his back tighter against his father's. They're steadily being surrounded by the enemy.

There's a cry from the Zodiacs and Logan sees that Brielle has fallen to the ground, a Skin standing over her with a gun in his hand. Tristan roars with rage, barreling into the man as if he's bulletproof. He knocks the Skin over and they both tumble to the ground, Tristan's fists pummeling the man over and over.

"Tristan!"

It's Jareth who calls out as he frantically fights off a Skin of his own. Logan's heart leaps into his throat when he sees that Veronica is being held by a third. Tristan is back by Jareth's side, bringing Brielle with him. The Skin roughly shoves Veronica at them and she stumbles into Jareth's arms.

A Skin, and then another, pull out guns and point them at the Zodiacs. Tristan and the others freeze.

They're losing, too. Because they can't use their suits or

their powers. If they do, then Logan's father has irrefutable proof.

But if they don't, then they're all dead.

"Bring them down here," a voice orders.

The Skins halt, seeing what Logan has. Solomon is standing beside the pod, the metal box tucked under his arm.

He smiles as he pats his hair back into place. "We might as well finish them all off at once."

The Skins at the other end of the warehouse close in around the Zodiacs, herding them toward Logan and his father. Solomon chuckles as his minions growl and sneer, the ones between Logan and the Zodiacs moving back, allowing their victims to come together.

All it takes is a few tense seconds and the Zodiacs are with Logan and Jack, forming a protective circle of their own.

They all face out, staring at the Skins they're now surrounded by. Some have guns. Some nurse little more than bloodlust, their faces full of the certainty that's all they need.

"Pitch," Tristan mutters beside Logan. "Their plan is a good one."

"Finish them," drawls Solomon.

"Take out the ones with guns first," shouts Tristan as the Skins launch into action.

Logan leaps at the nearest one, knocking the gun out of his hand before the Skin can shoot. The weapon clatters to the ground as Logan rams his elbow into the man's chest. His fist springs up, crushing the man's nose.

Behind him is a gunshot followed by the ping of a bullet hitting metal. Another failed attempt to kill a Zodiac.

It's only a matter of time before one hits its target.

Logan glances around, seeing his father fighting a Skin as another is running at him. Veronica is fighting with Jareth by her side. Tristan's foot connects with the side of a Skin's head, only for another to appear as the first crumples. Brielle is at his back, protecting it. Cassandra is a flurry of punches and kicks, and yet somehow, her gaze manages to connect with Logan's.

He senses everything she's feeling. Anger. Fear. Regret. And something sweet and warm, something that wants to be born...

Except they're surrounded. And even if his father was willing to run, the opportunity is gone. The Skins are like a well-oiled machine, slowly closing in on them.

The only way to survive is for the Zodiacs to be exposed.

All because the Zodiacs were protecting one of their own.

Logan.

As the Skins' cold determination pulses around him, Logan gets an idea. The machine of death surrounding them is about to be sabotaged.

Clenching his hands, he connects with the contained fury in the room. With the need to kill.

And amplifies it.

The first roar of rage comes from behind him. Tristan registers the crazed Skin running at Logan. He leaps forward, Brielle right there with him as if they're connected by an invisible rope, and knocks the man out.

Logan breathes in and then pushes the air out again, heating the bloodlust in the cavernous room. More Skins become a frenzy of movement as emotion overtakes reason. Cassandra ducks a wild punch, pushing up and driving her knee into the man's groin.

In the space of breath, the area becomes a cacophony of frenzied screams and furious roars. The Skins are now being controlled by aggression and violence, their strikes all about power but lacking a game plan. Each of the Zodiacs has enough fighting skills to dodge the crazy swings and wild surges. In fact, two Skins turn on each other when they get too close.

One by one, the Zodiacs incapacitate the Skins. There are only a few left when Tristan looks at Logan in surprise, as if he just realized what's happening. Logan nods, acknowledging he's the one doing this. Tristan raises a wry brow and opens his mouth to say something, possibly pointing out that a bunch of furious Skins isn't what he had in mind, but his face changes. His eyes widen with alarm, his gaze darting over Logan's shoulder. Before Logan can turn around, Tristan is moving.

Running toward Logan's father.

Tristan leaps at Jack and knocks him to the ground. The sound of a gunshot cracks a second later, the Skin who was not far behind falling to the ground with a cry.

The Skin with the gun, his eyes crazed with the need to kill, waves it from side to side as he tries to decide his next target.

"Die! All of you!" he screams.

Everyone stills. Logan drags in a breath and holds it, intent on trying to calm the man when the gun turns on him. Even that small movement was enough to gain the Skin's attention.

Except, then Cassandra is running. Sprinting. She's her very own bullet, aimed at the Skin.

The Skin sees the blur of movement, his aim changing trajectory. His hand tightens around the gun, his finger squeezing the trigger.

Logan sends out a jolt of the emotion screaming through him. The one that just froze his breath and scorched his veins.

The one that powers every cell as he runs toward Cassandra.

Fear.

There's a second of silence, a split moment of hesitation from the Skin. Which is all Logan needed.

His body slams into Cassandra's a second before the gunshot pierces the air. Pain punctures Logan's back a second before the world goes black.

CASSANDRA

Confusion has Cassandra spiraling when she and Logan hit the ground.

She heard the gunshot. She tries to deny the red soaking Logan's shirt as he lays in her arms, unmoving.

No, no, no.

She was supposed to take this bullet. Not him. Not him.

"No!" Jack roars, rushing to his son's side.

Cassandra looks up to see Brielle kick the gun out of the Skin's hand before he can fire another shot, and Tristan swoops in to tackle him to the floor.

Jack snaps his head up at Cassandra, snarling in anger and sorrow. "Why did he save you?"

No words come to Cassandra's lips. Logan's blood covers her hands, and her throat is so tight with grief that she can scarcely breathe.

Jack pulls Logan off Cassandra's lap and into his arms, cradling him. He presses his index and middle fingers to Logan's neck, and Cassandra watches intently.

"Oh, thank God he's still alive," Jack murmurs. He jerks

his head from side to side, opening his mouth as if to call out for help, but then closes it. There's no one left who can help.

Only two agents are left standing, and they're both locked in battle with Skins. As are the Zodiacs. But at least the numbers are evenly matched now. Six to six.

But she's still here, and she's going to save Logan if it's the last thing she does.

She gets to her feet, then extends both her hands to Jack. "Come on, we have to get him out of here."

Jack looks up at her, the same hatred still simmering in his eyes. But he doesn't refuse her help. He, too, will do anything to save his son.

He accepts her hands and together, they lift Logan up and head for the van.

She takes one last hesitant look over her shoulder at her friends. Tristan dispatches his opponent, snapping his neck and tossing him to the floor. He catches Cassandra's gaze, seeing the question there, and nods. Biting her lip, she faces forward and presses on even faster, determined to get Logan into the FBI van.

They manage to get Logan into the front passenger's seat and buckle him, then Jack slides into the driver's seat and Cassandra climbs into the cargo hold, gripping the back of Logan's chair as if it will somehow help him.

Jack flicks the key into the ignition, jerks the shaft into reverse and peels out of the warehouse through the hole Cassandra created. Neither of them say anything as Jack races down the road.

Cassandra's insides feel like they're being shredded apart. Logan jumped in front of a bullet for her. She'd intentionally taken the shooter's attention away from him so that he wouldn't get shot, but it happened anyway. Stupid boys! Hot tears sting her eyes, spilling over her eyelids and down her cheeks.

Please, let us get there in time. He can't die. Please!

After running multiple red lights and narrowly avoiding an accident that would have undoubtedly landed them all in the hospital, they come to a screeching halt at the entrance of the Emergency Room. Jack jumps out of the driver's seat and runs around to Logan's side as Cassandra kicks open the back doors and rushes to help him carry Logan out.

As they run into the lobby, nurses rush forward to meet them.

"What happened?" one of them asks.

"He was shot in the back," Jack says, his voice hoarse.

"We need a stretcher over here," the other nurse calls urgently toward the hallway, and soon two more nurses cart a long white stretcher their way.

They lay Logan down and immediately rush him down the hall.

"Are either of you relatives?" asks the chubby middle-aged nurse.

"I'm his father," Jack claims proudly, the wrinkles in his forehead showing his age.

The chubby nurse looks to Cassandra.

"I'm…uh…" She doesn't know how to respond.

"She's no one," Jack says, the words like a slap as he scowls at her.

"I'm sorry, honey," the nurse says, frowning at her. "You'll have to wait in the lobby."

"But—" Cassandra begins, but a fierce glower from Jack silences her. With the utmost reluctance, she lets go of the corner of the stretcher she'd been gripping so tightly and floats in the hallway, watching the only guy she's ever cared about disappear around the bend to an uncertain fate.

It feels like hours pass as Cassandra waits painfully in the lobby, rocking in the uncomfortable chairs, wringing her hands and bouncing her legs. Every now and then, she gets up to pace, and to ask the clerk at the front desk if there's been any news of Logan. Each time, the clerk just says she'll let Cassandra know as soon as he's out of surgery.

But even then, she may not be allowed to see him. And if he doesn't make it…

She doesn't let herself entertain that possibility. Logan has to live. He has to.

In between her bouts of worry, she tries to call the others. No one answers. Did they lose? Did more Skins show up and overpower them? Maybe she shouldn't have left them. She's a Zodiac Guardian. It's her duty to help her other Zodiacs. But Logan is a Zodiac too. And he needed her more than they did.

Although she'd be lying to herself if she believed that was the only reason she went with him.

She shouldn't have told him they were just teammates. What if that's the last thing she ever gets to say to him?

No! He's going to make it!

And why aren't any of them answering?

Frustration piles on to the worry and guilt, until her insides are a tangled knot of stress. Her entire body feels hot, not just her palms, and she's worried she may be glowing. She forces herself to take in long deep breaths and slowly blow them out, but that does little to calm her nerves or extinguish the fire that burns within her.

Finally, Jack emerges from the hallway, the wrinkles in his forehead angled in a decidedly disgruntled expression.

Fear makes her pop out of the chair like a tightly coiled spring, and she rushes to him.

"How is he?" she asks, desperation turning her question into a plea.

He scowls at her and she braces for the worst news.

"He wants to see you," Jack grumbles.

Elated relief blossoms through Cassandra, releasing the stress knot. She's so happy, she imagines she'll explode and splatter pieces of herself all over the walls and floor that the orderlies will never be able to fully clean up.

"Thank you," she peeps as happy tears blur her vision.

Jack turns around without acknowledging her and heads back down the hall. She follows him, practically skipping. He leads her to a room, then folds his arms and sits outside the open door, an unspoken invitation for her to go in alone.

Logan is laying upright in a hospital bed, his shirtless torso wrapped in bandages. His face brightens when he sees her, and that alone makes her heart squeeze.

"Are you alright?" he asks as she comes to sit next to the bed.

"You just got shot and you're asking me if I'm alright?" she counters.

He nods.

"I am now," she says, blinking away the film on her eyes. "Why did you jump in front of me?"

He takes one of her hands and squeezes it. "Because a Skin was about to shoot the woman I love."

She chokes on a hiccup as more tears force their way out. "Logan..."

"I know," he says. "I know that after everything, you don't feel the same way, but...I almost died. I'm not letting another minute go by without telling you how I feel."

She shakes her head, wiping her eyes. "You couldn't be more wrong. I—"

The song "Confident" by Demi Lovato blasts from her phone in her pocket. "Sorry," she says, reaching for it to silence it. But when she looks at the screen, she sees it's Brielle calling.

Filled with new desperation, she presses the phone to her ear. "Brielle?"

"Cassandra? Is Logan okay?" Brielle asks.

"Yes, he just got out of surgery. I think he's going to be okay. Are you guys okay? Why haven't you been answering my calls?"

"After we defeated the Skins, more agents showed up and detained us for ages."

Anger sparks in Cassandra's chest. Seriously? After we just saved two of their own and helped them fight the real bad guys?

"But they just released us and gave us our phones back," Brielle says.

"Good to see they finally came to their senses," Cassandra grouses. "What happened with Solomon and that weird box?"

Brielle pauses, and Cassandra knows it won't be good news. "He got away before the FBI showed up. The box is gone."

Cassandra sighs. She has no idea what that box is or what it can do, but if Chardis wants it, it must be extremely valuable. And they just lost it.

"We're heading your way now."

"Okay," Cassandra says, then hangs up.

She looks at Logan, a question in her eyes. "So the FBI had the others in custody, but just let them go."

Logan nods. "I told my dad that he was wrong about all of you. That there's nothing to investigate. We had a long talk, and it took a lot of convincing. He's not happy about it. But he can't refute that you guys helped us, that Tristan saved his life, and now that he's seen what the real bad guys are capable of…"

Cassandra lets all this sink in. She leans in closer. "You lied to him? For us?"

He squeezes the hand he's holding. "It wasn't exactly a lie. The Zodiacs aren't the criminals here. And if he stays on your trail, he really would be investigating the wrong people."

She meets his chocolate gaze, and she wants to melt into it. She leans against him, resting her head on his shoulder. "Is this okay?" she asks meekly.

"It's perfect," he says like a sigh, nuzzling his cheek against her forehead.

They sit like that for a long moment.

"I love you, too," she finally says, and he responds by kissing the top of her hair.

But then she pulls away. "How is this going to work?" she asks, feeling defeated. "Your dad is an FBI agent, and the head of the organization that wants to put us all behind bars."

"Jareth and Veronica make it work," he points out.

"Yes, and Veronica had to run away from home because being with a Zodiac means choosing us over her dad. Are you willing to do the same thing?"

"I'm not just with a Zodiac," he says. "I am one. And I'm going to find a way to make it so I won't have to choose."

She frowns at him dubiously. "How?"

He shakes his head. "I don't know yet. But we have to figure out how to show him that the Zodiacs are the good guys, and that Chardis and his Skins are the real villains."

"How are we going to do that?"

He reaches up to cup her cheek. "We'll find a way. I promise."

BRIELLE

The early October winds have brought in clouds, casting the afternoon in a lazy gray. The color mimics the way Brielle feels. Gray, with tints of bruised purple and somber blue.

She sits inside Creamy Dreams, waiting for Tristan to meet her.

The events of yesterday forced her to do some serious thinking, and she's not looking forward to the conversation she's about to have. But she knows it's the right decision. It has to be done.

The bell above the door rings, and Brielle looks up to see Tristan walking in with a smile. He looks so happy to see her.

Which only makes this harder.

"Hey there, beautiful," he greets, pecking her on the cheek before he sits beside her.

She plasters on a smile. "You seem especially cheerful today. How does it feel being back at the mansion?"

"It feels great!" he says with exuberance. "No more FBI on our backs, no more cramped attic—no offense." He chuckles, and she offers a weak laugh. "Although, I have to say, peanut butter and jelly sandwiches don't compare to Chef Brielle's cooking." He winks.

"Well, you know you're always welcome over for dinner any time," she says.

"Careful. I may be there every night. Speaking of delicious food, I'm gonna get a froyo. Want one?"

She shakes her head and he goes to the counter. Freedom is a good look on him. She hasn't seen him this happy in a long time. She hopes she's not about to steal that happiness.

He returns with a creamy concoction piled with gummy bears and M&Ms. "Have you heard anything from Cassandra or Logan?" he asks before spooning a small mountain into his mouth.

"They're still at the hospital," she answers. "Luckily the bullet missed his vital organs, but they're waiting to make sure the internal bleeding stops before they release him. Cassandra's been there all night and today."

"I'm sure Jack is thrilled about that," he says with one cheek stuffed.

Brielle scoffs. "You know Cassandra. I'm sure she'll charm him in no time."

"We can only hope. It'd be nice for Jack to like at least one of us." He digs in for another huge bite.

"I'm just glad Jack and Veronica smoothed things out," she adds, stalling. "It's too early for her and Jareth to run away together."

Tristan nods, crunching his M&Ms as he chews.

Swallowing, Brielle leans forward, resting her elbows on the table. "Look, Tristan…we need to talk."

He pauses mid chew, alarm crossing his face as he looks at her. He swallows. "What's up?"

She purses her lips and braids her fingers, forming her words carefully. "I don't think this is going to work," she says slowly, waving a hand back and forth between the two of them.

He props his spoon into his yogurt cup. "What do you mean?"

She sighs. "Yesterday, I thought I was going to lose everything outside of the Zodiacs. My home, my parents, my future. And it was so nice to know that you were there for me, no matter what."

His brow lowers questioning. "Of course. I'll always be here for you." He reaches forward to put a hand on hers.

"But you won't always be here for me in the way I need," she says, sheepishly pulling her hand away from his. She can't bring herself to look at him. "One day, you're going to find the other Gemini, and... Look, right now, with everything in our lives being uncertain, I just can't have our relationship being uncertain, too. I need at least one thing in my life to remain stable." She bites her lower lip. "The only way I can have that is if we stay just friends."

She slowly raises her eyes to gauge his reaction.

He looks shell-shocked. Like she just pulled the ground out from under him and he's falling to the Earth's core.

Regret instantly compels her to take it all back, to say she doesn't know what she's talking about. But her brain takes control and tightens the reins on her emotions. This really is what's best.

After the longest staring contest she could imagine, Tristan asks, "Is this because of what happened yesterday at HQ? Because—look, you have to know, I—"

She puts her hand up to stop him. "Please don't say anything we'll both regret." Her heart is breaking just as surely as his, and it's all she can do not to cry. She swallows down the urge. "Let's not think of this as breaking up. Let's just think of this as two best friends getting back together."

His eyebrows pucker upward in the most beautiful sad frown. "But what if I want more?"

"You can't give me more, and we both know it." Her breath catches in her throat, and if she says another word, she knows she's going to break down in so many ways.

Tristan's eyes plead with her to reconsider, but she can't stand it, so she looks away.

Finally, he leans back into his chair. "Okay." His voice is steely, guarded. Final.

She takes in a long breath through her nose, filling her lungs to give herself time to refresh. "I'll see you tomorrow."

He nods somberly, this time avoiding her gaze.

With nothing else left to say, she stands up and heads for the door.

It takes every ounce of her willpower to hold the tears at bay until she walks out the front door.

TRISTAN

Tristan flicks the lights off as he enters HQ. He retreated here the moment Brielle left Creamy Dreams, needing the darkness. The solitude.

He collapses into his chair, his bones aching like he just aged a century. The euphoria of their victory feels so long ago. It's as if it wasn't really a win at all. The fact he's here, alone, says it all.

He presses the heels of his palms into his eyes so hard he sees spots. He was going to say the words. The truth.

Give voice to what his heart has whispered over and over.

I love you, Brielle.

But he was too late. She just wants to be friends. What's worse, he can't be what she needs, not when he has a soulmate out there, waiting to be found.

"Zarius. Tess," he whispers. "I could really use you guys right about now."

But all that answers him is the low hum of technology. Lights wink from the control panels, the computer screens stare blankly at him.

There's nowhere for these emotions to go. All the confusion and pain can do is continue to jostle for first place. Tristan isn't sure which one is winning at any given moment.

"Some leader of the Zodiacs you are," he mutters to himself. "In love with the wrong girl. Kidding yourself that you have any idea what you're doing."

One of the screens comes to life, and Tristan almost turns his back on it. Can't the Universe give him a break for two secs?

He glances at it, his lifetime of training preventing him from turning away. The Zodiacs are the only ones standing between Chardis and Earth.

What he sees has him leaping to his feet and sprinting for the stairs.

He takes them two at a time, hoping he's not too late. He's only seen the car that just pulled into their driveway once, but he instantly recognized it. It was the black sedan. The one with the kid who's given him the thumb drives, cheerily waving to Tristan from the back window.

He needs to know who that kid is working for.

Slamming into the hallway wall, Tristan pushes off, digging his feet into the carpet. The doorbell rings—just the sort of thing the cheeky little gopher would do—as Tristan streaks past the living room.

He opens the door to the sound of tires squealing. Panting, he stands in the doorway as he watches the black car bounce off his driveway and onto the street.

"Pitch-freaking-dammit!" he shouts after it.

Tristan's about to take a step forward, a part of him considering running after the vehicle, when he sees something sitting on the front mat. A thumb drive.

He picks it up, frustrated that this has happened again. Another message from a mystery source. The Zodiacs don't need more unanswered questions in their lives.

Taking the thumb drive back down to HQ, he jabs it in

the port. Maybe it'll be good news. Maybe it's a congratulations on freeing Jack and finding the next Zodiac. Maybe it'll tell them what's in the box that Solomon has stolen...and how the pitch to get it back.

"Sure it will," Tristan mutters. "And maybe a unicorn will pop out and tell you how to get over Brielle."

The computer screen goes through the motions—blue, nothing for a nervous few seconds, virus scan complete. Tristan's eyes track the words that appear on his screen, his hand already reaching for the phone.

Message received through the wormhole. Code unknown.

Must be deciphered before it's too late.

He's going to have to pretend his pain and confusion don't exist. That his heart is happy to be 'just friends' with Brielle.

Because the Zodiacs need to get their asses here.

Right. Now.

Ready for the next installment in the Zodiac Guardians series? Check out VIRGO INCOGNITO!

VIRGO INCOGNITO

**Twelve teens. One task.
Save the Universe.**

Ada's always suspected she's not human. Bright and determined, she disappeared from society's radar the moment she could, using her hacking skills to survive.

And to keep searching for who or what she really is.

Eric, the soulful boy who ran away with her from the orphanage, is the only person she trusts. Their friendship is as deep as their love. Ada tells herself she doesn't need anything or anyone else.

When a coded message from Chardis is discovered, The Zodiacs reach out to Ada's online persona, Dyad, to decipher it. Tristan and the others promise they have the answers to her questions, an explanation for her inexplicable powers. Eric's willing to let them in.

But Dyad is wanted by the FBI. Ada can't afford to trust these teens she barely knows…can she? Even when the FBI's search for her becomes deadly. Even when she deciphers the ominous message.

Will Ada's mistrust cost her the family she's refused to let herself want? Or worse, will it cost her the only boy she's ever loved…

Grab your copy HERE!

http://mybook.to/VirgoIncognito

MORE EPIC ROMANCE TO FALL IN LOVE WITH!

ALSO BY TAMAR SLOAN

PRIME PROPHECY SERIES

KEEPERS OF THE GRAIL

KEEPERS OF THE CHALICE

KEEPERS OF THE LIGHT

KEEPERS OF EXCALIBUR

DESTINED DEMIGODS

ELEMENTAL GAMES

THE SOVEREIGN CODE

THE THAW CHRONICLES

ALSO BY TRICIA BARR

THE MATING GAMES

THE BOUND ONE SERIES

THE AMARANT SERIES

SHIFTER ACADEMY

HEAVENLY SINNERS

ABOUT THE AUTHORS

By day, Tricia is a full time mom to two beautiful girls and a wife/business partner to a handsome hard-working husband. By night—and nap times—she's a USA Today Best-selling Author of unique and thrilling teen and adult fantasies inspired by her vivid, somewhat creepy dreams and her own adventures around the world.

Tamar hasn't decided whether she's a psychologist who loves writing, or a writer with a lifelong fascination with psychology. She must've been someone pretty awesome in a previous life (past life regression indicates a Care Bear), because she gets to do both. When not reading, writing, or working with teens, Tamar can be found with her husband and two sons enjoying country life in their small slice of the Australian bush.